Impossibly YOURS

AJ RANNEY

Impossibly YOURS

AJ RANNEY

Rudy House Publishing

Impossibly Yours

Half Moon Lake Book Two

Developmental Edit by Katie Bockino

Line, Copy, Proofreading by Beth Lawton at VB Edits

Interior formatting by H.C. PA & Formatting Services

Cover by K. B. Barrett Designs

ISBN: **979-8-9859485-4-7** (ebook)

ISBN: **979-8-9859485-5-4** (paperback)

 Created with Vellum

For Jenn—even though Ashley isn't your favorite,
I still appreciate all the feedback, line edits,
and conversations you endured to help make her story even
better.

Chapter One

JACKSON

"ANOTHER." I rubbed the back of my neck and took in the room full of stupidly happy people, sliding the low-ball glass toward the bartender.

He arched a brow. "Shouldn't you be celebrating the lovely couple, not drowning your sorrows at the bar by yourself?"

"It's been a shit week, man. Just give me another one." I pinched my eyes closed in hopes of clearing my head. Then I downed another drink and pushed away from the bar.

I scanned the linen-covered tables. According to Bella and Ashley, the tablecloths were ivory, not white. They looked white to me, but I wasn't about to argue with the bride or her maid of honor.

A warm gust blew in from the lake, and I inhaled the mossy air that was infused with just a hint of pine. The glow from the lights lining the edge of the tent stood out against the dark sky. North Carolina's constant summer rain forced the just-in-case tent, but it had turned out to be a beautiful September night.

I loosened the bow tie that had me in a death grip. The damn things always choked me. I fucking hated monkey suits. This was my best friend's wedding, though, so I wouldn't complain, but I would have preferred something a lot less formal. A pair of well-worn pants and a dress shirt with the sleeves rolled was usually as fancy as I got. But as the best man, I did as I was told and wore the damn tux.

We hadn't always been close. Rhett Williams had been the quarterback of the high school football team when my family relocated from New York when I was sixteen. If we hadn't been paired as lab partners and connected over our shared interest in playing guitar, we probably wouldn't have become friends. And although we'd been tight for years, I couldn't help but wonder if he would've asked me to be his best man if his older brother Kyle wasn't currently deployed overseas.

My steps echoed against the floor as I made my way toward my mother. She winced, trying to push herself up from the chair she had settled into only five minutes ago. She'd spent too much time on her feet between the ceremony and the reception, and it was taking its toll.

"What the fuck is she doing?" I muttered. She needed to take it easy, *not* overdo it. She had pushed herself too hard all summer, which meant I'd had to cancel an important business trip scheduled for next week so I could be here to help her. Her surgery to repair the herniated disc wasn't *originally* planned until after the holidays, and even though my father, my sister, and I had offered to help her all summer, she was too proud to let us. Now she had no choice.

"Why don't you and Dad go home?" I grabbed her elbow to support her as she stood. Pain radiated through her tight smile. Her back had been a constant issue over the last year, and she couldn't stand the pain medication. In her mind, the loss of control she experienced when she took them far outweighed the pain-free hours.

Ridiculous.

"I can't leave yet. Rhett and Bella are still here. And I need to help Ashley make sure everything gets broken down and packed up in the van. If it's not done right, it'll be a mess to sort." She took half a step around me but hissed as her back gave out.

"Mom. *Sit down*," I urged, clutching her elbow again and trying to stay calm.

For the first time, I noticed the strands of gray hair and wrinkles that lined her forehead and breathed a sigh of relief at the surrender written all over her face.

My mother was one of the most stubborn people I knew. Well, maybe aside from her apprentice, Ashley. I swear the two of them wore me out—I was trying to get one to let me do what she'd asked of me and the other to accept the help I'd been asked to give.

It was probably time to let the catering business go, and even though I'd told my mom that twice now, she wasn't ready. She had started it because she enjoyed cooking, creating the menus, and planning events, but if she couldn't do much of that anymore, what was the point of keeping it? It wasn't even lucrative.

"Look, I got this. I'll help Ashley tonight." I'd already told her this earlier. "Go home and get off your feet." They'd moved her surgery up and wanted her to take it easy for the next two weeks.

Over my mom's shoulder, I locked eyes with my dad, who was heading toward us. He nodded as understanding passed between us. When he muttered something in Spanish, I knew he must have witnessed the same thing I had. Unless we were in Texas visiting his side of the family, he rarely pulled out his native tongue. And when he did, it was because he was frustrated.

"Time to go, Barbara." My dad's no-nonsense tone and my mom's sigh confirmed things. They were finally leaving.

"I'll find Ashley and see where she needs help." I bent down and placed a brief kiss on her cheek before turning to walk away.

"Make sure you load the van correctly!" she called after me.

"Yes, Mother." Because, of course, I never did anything right. I was the eternal bachelor who didn't truly have his shit together at thirty, according to my parents. In their minds, my success was merely a fluke rather than hard earned. My jet-setting lifestyle and casual relationships only enforced the irresponsible and unreliable image of me they'd created.

What most people didn't understand? I wasn't willing to settle. I worked hard for my success, no matter what others thought. And *I* was proud of it. But over the last year, I'd slowly gotten sick of the meaningless relationships. For a few years after some bad experiences, casual was what I wanted, but now? I was ready for more. Finding it had been the problem. The women I'd met were of two types. Each one either had a great personality, but we lacked chemistry, or the sex was great, but I couldn't stand to be in the same room with the chick while fully clothed.

I'd heard the rumors, knew what everyone thought. I'd been labeled the town's rich playboy. Letting people think what they wanted to was easier than constantly trying to prove them wrong.

It didn't help that my parents were well off. People that didn't know me assumed that my money was handed to me. They saw the tattoos, my financial status, the lack of a regular nine-to-five, and a revolving door of women and made assumptions.

Just like the situation with Sophia. A child I desperately wanted to help but could only do so much for. And as hard as I fought, it was never enough. I failed. I failed *her*. Would the outcome have been the same if I were a woman?

Probably not. Because let's face it, I didn't fit the image the courts expected to see of a *responsible adult.*

I balled my hands into fists as I replayed the meeting I'd had with my lawyer.

But no, I couldn't go there. Not now. Not yet.

Lost in my thoughts, I rounded the corner of The Dock, the Williams family's restaurant, inn, and marina. I didn't see Ashley until it was too late, and I collided with her, sending the trays she'd had balanced in her arms crashing to the ground. At least I'd grabbed her arm to steady her on her heels before she toppled over with them.

"God dammit, Jackson. What the hell is wrong with you?" The fire in her azure eyes seared my skin as she glared at me. Though the fury didn't detract from the perfect way she filled out the dress that matched the color of her eyes and the vest I wore over my white tuxedo shirt.

"Sorry, I wasn't paying attention."

"Why am I not surprised? Do you *ever* consider *anyone* but yourself?" She yanked out of my hold and bent to pick up the trays. Her pinned-up blond hair bounced slightly, threatening to topple free.

Do not lose your cool. Do not lose your cool.

"Said I was sorry. Here, let me." I scooped the trays up and headed toward the van but paused mid-step and turned to face her. "You know, there're employees here to load this stuff up.

Shouldn't you be enjoying the rest of your *brother's* wedding?"

She clenched her jaw and crossed her arms. "Your mother likes the van loaded a certain way. I'm just making sure it's done right."

How these two worked together, I had no clue. They were both stubborn in their own ways.

"Who's going to unload it tomorrow? It won't be my mom; I can guarantee that. She overdid it tonight."

"And it sure as hell won't be you. Like you'd bother to get up early on a Sunday to help me."

"Because you know me so well?" I gripped the trays tighter, my biceps and forearm muscles tightening, but let out a deep breath, hoping once more to reason with the woman who seemed intent on driving me to drink. "Look, let's enjoy the rest of the wedding. Miguel and Kelly will load up the van. I'll be there tomorrow at eight to help you unload it. Promise."

"Why am I not surprised you would want to pass the work off on other people?"

"We *pay* them! It's their job! Jesus Christ."

My attention landed on Kelly, our head server, as she made her way toward us.

"Let me take those." Kelly gestured to the trays I was still clutching. "You guys should go back out there. They're looking for you two. Something about a final dance with the whole wedding party." She nodded in the direction she had come from, then moved toward the van.

"You and Miguel know how to load the van the way my mom likes it, correct?" I asked.

Kelly's tight smile was answer enough. "Of course. That's one of the first things Mrs. Vargas and Miss Williams trained us to do."

"I've told you to call me Ashley," she huffed.

"Thank you, Kelly." I gripped Ashley by the elbow and turned her back toward the white tent. "Come on. Put your fake smile on and pretend you don't hate me while we dance."

"I'm not *that* good an actress," she sneered.

Even though I tried to stop it, the corner of my mouth twitched. "Well, for the sake of our best friends, I'm sure you can fake enjoying a five-minute dance with me."

"I bet you're very familiar with women faking with you."

I couldn't help it this time. I threw my head back and laughed. This girl had balls. Never one to back down and always determined to get in the last word. It was one of the reasons I'd spent the better part of the last fourteen years riling her up; I knew she'd throw it right back at me.

I shook my head. "Nope, their screams are always a hundred percent pure satisfaction. The only faking I've experienced has to do with personalities. They turn on the charm when they think I can give them the lifestyle they want. It's why I make it clear that all they'll get from me are mind-blowing orgasms and nothing more."

And with that, she was finally speechless.

Fuckin' A.

Chapter Two

JACKSON HAD SWORN he'd be here at eight, but it came as no surprise that he was nowhere to be found. When it came down to it, he only cared about himself, his bank account, and his next hookup. I went to college with guys just like him. Spoiled trust fund brats who couldn't give a damn about anyone but themselves. Just like Paul, who'd been too self-centered to care about what I wanted but knew how to turn on the charm as he fed me whatever bullshit he thought I wanted to hear in the moment. My ex was skilled at manipulating me, and I'd happily let him because I'd convinced myself if I did enough or tried hard enough, he would care more.

Shaking myself from my thoughts, I turned and took a step before the stacked items I was holding tipped.

"Fuck," I screamed as the container of serving utensils landed on my foot. Dropping the two other bins on the floor of the van, I tried not to lose my shit.

Who could have predicted I'd be unloading this crap alone this morning? Oh right. I did.

I'm going to kill him.

Hunched over with my hands on the tops of my thighs, I ground my teeth and breathed deeply through my nose, trying unsuccessfully to ignore the throbbing in my big toe.

"You know, if you would have trusted me to be here like I said I would, this wouldn't have happened," Jackson mumbled from somewhere at my feet.

I watched him gather the utensils and place them back in the container. Two paper coffee cups and a takeout bag sat on the ground, snagging my attention.

But I refused to give him the upper hand. To admit that yes, in fact, I had assumed he that he wouldn't show. That I'd spent the last twenty minutes cursing his name. His existence. His mom's lack of trust in me. Her desire to stick me with her lazy-ass son who didn't understand what hard work was. Must be nice to sit back, throw money at people, and call it a day.

I blinked, bringing my attention back to Jackson, who stood to his full height. He was at least half a foot taller than my five-seven, and his white T-shirt covered a very solid, muscular chest, while the intricate patterns of a tattoo wove just under the collar and disappeared down into his shirt. His dark features, from his hair to his almost black eyes, gave a whole new meaning to the phrase tall, dark, and handsome.

My throat went dry at the sight. I licked my lips but jutted my chin in a show of defiance when a cocky smirk broke out across Jackson's face. It was bad enough that he had this sexy *bad boy* edge that *all* the women flocked to, but he knew it, and that was what really aggravated me. He *knew* he had that

9

effect on every female he came in contact with. And I cursed my lack of immunity.

"You're late," I spat.

"I stopped for coffee and donuts. *You're welcome.*"

"You probably don't care if you waste my time, but I do."

He shrugged. "Yeah, okay. It was like five minutes."

"No, it's been twenty."

"Whatever. I'll buy a watch," he said in an *I don't give a shit* tone.

I huffed and grabbed the container of utensils out of his hands. Of course he wouldn't understand. Not sure why I even tried, but at least he wasn't pretending he gave a damn.

Turning, I headed for the back door to the catering office. Jackson was hot on my heels as I made my way into the large commercial-grade kitchen and set the box down. Blessedly, the phone rang as I was turning around, giving me the perfect temporary escape.

Walking down the long hallway, I passed the storage area on the left, then turned into my office to answer the phone. I needed a minute to pull myself together. As much as I hated his pretentious ass, my treacherous body hadn't gotten the memo. Like that night six months ago when I drank too much at the bar and he insisted on giving me a ride home. So I got in his car and instantly regretted it as my body hummed with desire.

When I returned to the kitchen after dealing with the telemarketer, I was reminded yet again of why I couldn't stand this man.

"What. Are. You. Doing?" I asked, putting both hands on my hips.

"Um—having breakfast?" He raised one eyebrow and motioned to the other coffee and donut set out on the large kitchen island.

"Can we just get this done? You've already set us back

twenty minutes." I took a breath in through my mouth to avoid the delicious scent of the coffee he'd brought with him.

"Yep. As soon as I finish." He raised the donut to his mouth and took a slow, dramatic bite. Why was he always such an ass? "Don't be a brat. It's pumpkin spice." He nodded to the cup in front of me on the island.

"How—"

Did he know that was the only fancy coffee flavor I'd drink?

"It's just a cup of coffee. You can go back to hating me afterward." He crowded my space, the cup in his outstretched hand.

I had overslept that morning and had skipped brewing myself a mug. I hated being late for anything. Apparently, Jackson didn't feel the same way. He didn't care if he inconvenienced others.

But.

I *really* wanted that coffee. *Damn* him.

"You're an asshole." I snatched the drink from his hand. "But thanks."

"I know." The corner of his mouth turned up as he winked at me. "And you're welcome."

I walked over to the counter and grabbed the donut he'd set on a napkin. How Jackson ate donuts and looked like that I couldn't understand.

"Can you email me the schedule for the next two weeks?"

"What—Why?" I stuttered.

"So I know when and where I need to be?" He articulated each word like I was hard of hearing.

"I'm confused."

"I'm shocked." He chuckled.

"No. I thought you weren't taking over for your mom until she goes in for surgery."

"That was the original plan, but you saw her last night.

She overdid it again." He huffed, narrowing his eyes at me. "So she's done, and you get me."

Great. Just fucking great. I'd been doing my best to accept all the changes coming down the pike. First Barbara's approaching surgery, and then the declaration that Jackson would be stepping into her role. Even though I didn't need the help. And now? Now the timeline had changed, yet no one had thought to mention it to me. I was expected to just roll with it.

Okay. Deep breath.

I'm fine. It's fine. I've got this.

"I don't need your help." Calm. Nice. I could do this. "We only have a few events scheduled over the next few weeks; I've got it covered."

"No doubt you do. But that's not the plan."

"Really, I—" I began before he interrupted—another one of his endearing qualities.

"I don't want to do this either, but just send it to me, or I'll ask my mother to do it."

I matched his glare with one of my own. But what could I have said? He *was* the owner's son. I tightened my grip on my coffee to give myself a moment to formulate a response.

"Fine. Whatever. But don't complain about which events I give you."

The women's dinner at the church was coming up. It was always the last Sunday of the month. I'd be happy to give him that one.

"Fuck," he mumbled.

I couldn't help but smirk as I spun away from him. He didn't have quite as much control here as he'd thought.

From the fridge, I grabbed the tomatoes, onions, basil, and garlic while sipping on my coffee. I loved fall and anything pumpkin, so I savored the flavor.

"What are you doing?" Jackson's brows knitted together.

"Prepping the bruschetta for the luncheon tomorrow." I picked up a serrated knife and pointed toward the back hallway. "*You* can finish unloading the van."

"Are you always this bossy?" He popped the rest of his donut into his mouth and pushed away from the counter. "What pasta did they choose? I'll work on the sauce after I unload the van."

Uh... *he* would make the sauce? Barbara promised Jackson would be helpful because he knew his way around the kitchen better than his sister Brittney, but I assumed I would do most of the cooking while Jackson assisted with the prep work.

I tried to school my features. Maybe he was just good at following directions. I didn't need Barbara's sauce recipes anymore. I didn't need the instructions. My mom said my memory for detail and my skill at recognizing certain flavor profiles were what made me good at cooking.

"Um—alfredo, I think. I have the recipe around here somewhere."

Before I could set the knife down to go in search of it, his words stopped me.

"I don't need it. I've been cooking with my mom since I was little. Know all her recipes by heart." And with that, he walked away, leaving me standing there with my mouth hanging open.

Damn him, I repeated to myself over the next hour as I cut the tomatoes, onions, and basil and sealed them individually in airtight containers.

The garlic was sautéing in the olive oil on the stove when Jackson carried in the last items from the van. I would combine all the ingredients tomorrow morning and toast the bread squares before Miguel loaded everything up and delivered it.

Jackson grabbed a large sauce pot and took the spot next to me. Leaning over, he inhaled the aroma coming from my pan.

"You need more garlic," he said.

"I do *not* need more garlic." I had the urge to hit him over the head with the spoon I was holding. What, he thought he was an expert now?

Cocky asshole.

He cocked a brow and shrugged. "Just trying to help."

"I'm not done yet anyway. I need to add my secret ingredient."

"What is it? Oregano?" When I just smiled and didn't answer, he continued. "Red pepper? Rosemary?"

I shrugged and bit the inside of my cheek when he leaned over my shoulder to examine the ingredients I had spread out on the counter. I breathed in the hints of sage and lavender that wafted from him.

"Thyme?"

"What?" I stuttered, my brain foggy in such close proximity to him.

He nodded to the fresh thyme sprigs to my left. "That's your secret ingredient. Smart. But you still need more garlic."

I rolled my eyes, and we worked silently until I tasted the olive oil and silently cursed. He was right. I still needed more garlic. He chuckled when I added a pinch more.

"Shut up," I mumbled.

There was no way I could work side by side with this man for the next three months. He'd drive me crazy. Our work styles didn't mesh. Hell, *we* didn't mesh. Maybe I could make a schedule. Then I could use the kitchen some days, and he'd have free rein the other days. Each of us would prepare for the events we were taking on, never having to cross paths.

. . .

I PULLED up to Rhett and Bella's small mountain cabin that overlooked Half Moon Lake. Bella was like a sister to me, and since she'd married my brother Rhett two weeks ago, I could officially call her that. They'd gotten their second chance and were now a family of three with Bella's son Brendan.

I mentally prepared myself before getting out of the car. Five years ago, she and I both would've bet I'd be the one married by the time we were twenty-eight, not her. Especially given that I was in a serious relationship with thoughts of getting married at the time, while Bella continued to avoid her feelings for my brother.

I was happy for Bella, so I wouldn't call it jealousy, but it was hard to swallow the notion that she'd gotten here first. Not that I wanted that life anymore. And I wasn't sure I would ever want it again. I needed to deal with my shit first, but that was tomorrow's problem.

A two-year-old's naked rear end greeted me as I opened the front door, interrupting a standoff between mom and son. Bella was poised with crossed arms and a glare that put my mom's to shame. Our eyes locked, and at the slight twitch of her lips, my money was on her. The toddler was done for.

"I guess Aunt Ashley doesn't get to read you your bedtime stories tonight since you refuse to put your pajamas on," Bella said, shaking her head, her mouth turning down into a frown.

"Nooo!" Brendan whined. "You mean, Mama!" He turned to me with hope in his eyes. "I wear PJs and I get bedtime stories?"

I nodded toward Bella. "Listen to Mama, little man."

"You ready to put your pajamas on now?"

"Okay." He surrendered and walked down the hallway toward his room. Bella rolled her eyes before she followed him, making me chuckle. But witnessing this power struggle cemented my desire not to have kids anytime soon.

I put the wine I brought on the counter and went through the steps to uncork it and pour us each a glass.

"Aunt Assey!"

I spun around in time to scoop a now fully clothed Brendan into my arms. "Now that's better, isn't it?"

"Me not like clothes."

I barked out a laugh. I couldn't blame the kid. He ran into the other room after I set him down. How Bella kept up with the little ball of energy, I had no clue.

"I was excited when I bought this outfit. Now I'm afraid I won't get him into it," Bella said, holding up the cutest pants, button-down shirt, and bow tie.

"How'd you get him to wear the suit for the wedding?"

"No idea. He got ready with the guys. They probably bribed him." She laughed, the corners of her eyes crinkling.

"What's the outfit for?" I racked my brain for what special event was coming up. Thanksgiving was still almost two months away.

"The adoption hearing, remember? You promised you'd be there."

"Crap. Yes, I remember now. Did they set a date yet?"

"No. We're waiting for our marriage certificate. The attorney said once we file, we'll get the date. It should be sometime before Christmas."

We grabbed our wineglasses and moved into the living room, watching Brendan play with trucks and cars while we sat on the sofa.

"So the honeymoon was good?" I asked.

"It was amazing." A smile spread across her face, and a blush flooded her cheeks. "Lots of practice."

I stopped the glass halfway to my lips and tilted my head. "Practicing for what?" I asked, then took a sip of my wine.

"Making a baby."

I coughed, choking on the wine. "Say what?" I sputtered.

Her smile said it all. "We don't want to wait too long to give B a sibling, but I just stopped my birth control, so it'll probably take a few months."

"Aw, Bella, I'm so freaking happy for you two." I hugged my best friend.

"Thanks." Bella tried to hide her smirk behind her wineglass as she took a sip. "I see you and Jackson haven't killed each other yet."

"Well, that might be speaking too soon. I almost did two days ago when he called me *princess* again for the billionth time. I've asked him to stop, but he does whatever he wants. Probably because it pisses me off."

"I would venture to say that's a good guess." She raised one eyebrow at me. "I don't get why you let him rile you up so much. You have two older brothers and you don't let *them* get to you the way Jackson does."

"I know what you're doing." I scowled into my wineglass. "But it's not like that. We really can't stand each other. Do you know what he said to me at the office the other day?"

"Hmm?"

"That he needed to teach me how to be a *thriftier* spender. He was livid that I bought high-top pub tables at three hundred a pop."

"How many did you get?"

"Twelve."

Her eyes went round. "You know he's not wrong, though, right? I told you that when you were looking at them. You could probably find them somewhere else for half the price."

"I know. But I like the ones I picked out." I crossed my arms, feeling defensive. "They're better quality, and they came with a storage cart."

What upset me the most was that he didn't even ask. Like he just assumed I hadn't put any thought or research into the

17

purchase. His mom had approved them, but he didn't seem to care about that information.

When Bella's silence became too much, I added, "He can just deal. It's not his business. When I told him to go to hell, he called me a frustrating spoiled brat."

Bella threw her head back and laughed.

I rolled my eyes. "Glad you find his assholeyness so funny."

"Only because you guys bicker like a married couple."

"Daddy!" Brendan squealed.

The loud rumble of Rhett's truck followed by headlights shining through the large bay windows sent Brendan flying toward the door.

"Don't you dare step foot out that door! You just had a bath. Wait until he comes in."

"*But...*" he whined, hopping from one foot to another in anticipation.

I bit back a laugh at the adorable look on Brendan's face. His eyes sparkled with excitement and his bottom lip stuck out in a pout.

"Hey, little man," Rhett said as he came through the front door and scooped the toddler into his arms. "Did you miss me?"

"*Yes*! Mama too."

"Is that right?" Rhett said, locking eyes with his wife, a smile tugging at his lips.

"Trains?" Brendan asked Rhett.

Rhett raised his eyebrows at Bella. "If Mama says it's okay."

"Yes. Twenty minutes, and then Aunt Ashley can read him his bedtime stories."

"Okay." Rhett bent and placed a chaste kiss on Bella's lips as he passed.

In that moment, my heart yearned for someone to look at

me the way Rhett looked at Bella, for a partnership like they had. But how could I trust myself to find someone trustworthy enough to rely on the way she did with him? I missed all the red flags in my last relationship. Was I ready to try again? Not likely, but it didn't stop my stupid heart from longing for it.

Chapter Three

JACKSON

I BRACED my hands on the kitchen island and shook my head at the most recent container of food that had been dropped off. It had been a little over two weeks since I'd taken over for my mom. Callahan's Classic Events had been my mom's passion for the last twelve years. When she first showed me the space she picked out for the business, she had been happy to finally have something of her own. This business meant so much to her, and that was why I'd agreed to help.

Neither of my parents *needed* to work anymore. They had both come from money, and with my father's career as an investment banker on Wall Street, they were more than comfortable. My dad still dabbled in investing, mostly stocks, but he was becoming more and more interested in the type of investing I'd been doing.

After my father's heart attack and the fast-paced life we'd lived in New York, my parents had been happy to leave the hustle and bustle of a big city. At sixteen, though, it had been hard for me to see past my anger at being forced to move away from the only home I'd ever known. But luckily, music became my outlet. And in many ways, it still was.

A knock at the door brought me back to the present. I pushed away from the counter in my parents' kitchen and made my way to the door. If it was another elderly lady bringing a meal, I was going to lose it. Damn, how many fucking casseroles did we need? It was just my mom and dad. And Dad knew how to cook. Maybe not as well as my mom, but he could throw shit together.

I plastered on a smile and opened the door. "Oh, it's you. What are you doing here?"

Ashley rolled her eyes. "Hi." Her voice was *too* perky.

I dragged a hand through my hair. "Don't tell me you brought a casserole, because I will slam the door in your face."

"Nope. I signed up for Friday. I did bring Barbara her favorite cupcakes, though," she said, holding up a bakery box.

I stepped out of the way to allow her to come inside. "Signed up for what?"

"The meal train. My mom organized it."

I followed her through the house until we reached the kitchen. "I still have no fucking clue what you're talking about. What the hell is a meal train?"

"Do you seriously know nothing? It's a schedule created for people who want to bring meals by. Everyone signs up for a day."

"That's ridiculous. Why would anyone think that was a good idea?" I realized a moment too late that her mom probably did since she organized it.

Ashley just tilted her head and scowled.

I cleared my throat. "Well, whatever. Thank you, I guess,

but it really isn't needed. My mom is barely eating, and when she does, we get whatever it is she's craving. Want to know what my parents ate for dinner last night?"

"Not really. But I have a feeling you're going to tell me anyway."

"Chinese. My mom hasn't had an appetite and just wanted fried rice."

"She doing okay? In a lot of pain? Or nauseous from the meds?"

"She's a horrible patient. And yes, nauseous when she takes the pain meds, and then in pain when she refuses."

"Sounds like Barbara."

I rubbed the back of my neck to ease the tension there. "Yeah, she's too damn stubborn. But I can't blame her. I didn't like taking those types of drugs either after the car accident."

"I remember that..." She tucked her hair behind her ears and glanced away. "Your mom was beside herself. You're lucky you walked away with only a few broken bones."

I shrugged. I didn't like talking about the accident—wasn't even sure what made me bring it up to begin with. "Probably. But it was worth it. My nurse was hot as fuck. We went out a few times once I was back on my feet, and the things she did with her mouth—"

"Just stop. Jesus, why are you like this?" Her glare tore through me, and she crossed her arms.

Mission accomplished. I moved to the counter and picked up the container of food I'd left sitting there. I stood in front of the open refrigerator, trying to figure out where to put it. The casseroles had taken up every available inch of space. "Are you hungry?"

"Um, what?"

"Food. You know, the stuff you eat?" I grabbed the chicken, broccoli, and rice casserole and tossed it onto the island, then put the newest meal in its spot. I shook my head at the insanity of this meal train idea.

"Yes, *asshole*. I know what food is. I was hoping I could visit with your mom for a bit. Is she resting?"

"Yeah. We convinced her to take her pain pills an hour ago. It's really the only time she sleeps. Why don't you hang around, have something to eat? She doesn't usually nap more than a couple of hours." I followed the directions on the tin lid covering the casserole, preheating the oven to the stated temperature, then leaned against the counter, arms crossed. "We have to chat anyway."

"About what?" she asked, pursing her lips.

"The events this weekend. I'm taking the donor dinner at the hospital on Friday. You'll do the other thing on Saturday night."

"What? No way." She slammed her hands to her hips.

She was already trying my patience. Ashley was used to getting her way. With everyone. But this was her wake-up call because that bullshit wouldn't work with me.

"I wasn't asking. My mom handed over control of the company to me while she's out. You wouldn't push back if she was the one making this change, and you're not gonna do it with me either. Understand?"

I could almost see the steam coming out of her ears as her cheeks heated to a nice shade of red. She really hated to be forced out of her pretty little box of control.

"The difference is that your mom respects me and would never ask me to give up one of our biggest events. Especially because *I've* done all the legwork."

She crossed her arms and turned away the instant the words left her mouth, her shoulders slumping and her fingers digging into her arm.

Fuck. I wasn't trying to be an asshole. I just didn't want to attend the fucking donor dinner as a guest, and it would look bad if two donors from the same family didn't show up. My dad needed to be at home with mom. I would make an appearance, but if I was managing the catering staff, then I wouldn't have to mingle.

"Fine, we'll both work Friday, then. If it's that big, it might be best to have both of us there anyway."

She spun back to me, her eyes burning with anger. At least the spitfire was back.

"If you think I'm working all weekend just because you have pussy lined up on Saturday night, you have another thing coming."

I threw my hands up; I couldn't win with her. I hadn't done anything for myself in the last two weeks. I made food and ran the events she assigned to me. "This is the van thing all over again. You assume the worst—that I'm going to bail."

I clenched my jaw and slid the casserole into the oven. Turning back toward her, I crossed my arms and braced for what she was going to say next.

"Hey," my sister Brittney said as she entered the kitchen. Her head swiveled from me and then to Ashley and back while we continued to glare at each other, neither of us willing to back down. "Um, am I interrupting?"

"Just your brother being a controlling ass."

Why was Ashley always so confrontational? I was good at reading women, but damn, I couldn't figure her out to save my life. Her hatred toward me had been worse lately. Maybe she *did* remember what happened when I drove her home from the bar back in April and was just too proud to admit it. We had never spoken of that moment, and I sure as hell didn't want to now either. Sweat rolled down my back, though, as I wondered what she could recall from that night.

Ashley said a few more words to Brittney before turning to leave. Once the front door shut, I relaxed my jaw and turned at the sound of my sister clearing her throat. Her dark brown eyes that matched mine perfectly studied me.

"Don't start," I bit out.

"I didn't say anything... but I'm going to say I told you so once you guys finally hook up."

"Nope, never gonna happen. I told you already; she hates me."

"I didn't say she liked you. Girls hook up with guys they don't like all the time."

I shook my head at my little sister. "And you know that from experience?" I threw my hand up, palm out, cutting off any response she may have given me. "You know what? Don't answer that."

She huffed out a laugh before pressing her lips together and shaking her head. "Wait, you said *she* hates *you*... but you didn't deny wanting her. You do, don't you?"

"She's my best friend's sister. It's not happening."

"You're still not saying no."

"What do you want from me? Is she hot? Yup. I'm not denying that. But she hates me, and most days I barely tolerate her. And she's Rhett's sister, which makes her off-limits. Can we please change the subject now?"

For years, I'd tried, and most of the time succeeded, to ignore how attractive she was. Why cause myself headaches? Then, when I took her home that night months ago, something shifted between us. For the first time, I wondered what it would be like to kiss her. To touch her. And that fucking floored me, knowing I couldn't let myself go there with her. But lately, it had been harder to ignore the chemistry bubbling just under the surface between us.

Brittney opened her mouth and then slammed it shut, pausing before finally asking, "What's in the oven?"

"A chicken and rice casserole. Do you know what a meal train is?"

"Like a schedule of when people are going to drop off food to people who need it?"

"Exactly!" I stabbed the air with my index finger. "*Need*. Not our parents. Shit, they could hire someone to come in and cook for them for the next four weeks if they wanted."

"Yeah, but they wouldn't. And Mom will appreciate the sentiment, even if it's not needed. But it does seem like a waste, I guess."

"Hope you like chicken, broccoli, and rice, 'cause that's what's for dinner."

"Sounds good."

"Hey... I thought you couldn't get here until the weekend."

My sister had lived and worked in Asheville since she graduated from college a few years ago, but she was good about coming home frequently.

"I took a few days of PTO. Someone from the Nashville office is coming to take over next week since the owners are stepping away from the company until they can finally settle their nasty divorce. Figured I should take the time before the new guy steps in." Brittney shrugged and picked at her nails.

Something was amiss, and I wanted to kick myself for not noticing the moment she walked in. Even though she was five years younger than me, we'd always been close, and I could read her better than anyone else in my life.

"What's up with you? Something wrong?"

Her head popped up, her eyes wide. "Shit, is it that noticeable?"

"Only because I know you so well."

"I was stupid; I did something I've never done before and got burned."

"You're not stupid. Whatever it was, I've probably done worse. Or will at some point." I shrugged and crossed one foot over the other and rested more solidly against the counter at my back.

"Have you ever... hooked up with a girl and left before she woke up?"

"You had a one-night stand and snuck out on the poor schmuck?" I couldn't help but gasp. This was my sweet, thoughtful little sister.

"No, you idiot. Well, yes and no. I guess it was a one-night stand, but he was gone when I woke up and never gave me his number or his last name or anything. He acted like he was into me, and I thought we really hit it off." Her mouth formed a tight line, and her eyes blazed with anger. "If I ever see him again, I'm going to knee him in the balls."

"You didn't know him at all? Like he was a complete stranger?" My sister had never been reckless like that. It was usually my MO.

"Yeah, I know—stupid—okay, let's change the subject."

My phone vibrated against the counter, and I grabbed it. But I clenched my jaw and considered throwing the damn thing when I read the display.

"Goddamn woman," I mumbled.

"Who?"

"Ashley. She ordered these expensive-ass serving pub tables, and now she expects me to be there tomorrow to accept the delivery."

"Tell *her* to do it. You can't let her walk all over you."

I ran my hand over the back of my neck and hid a smirk. "Well—she has an event at the same time the tables are scheduled for delivery."

Brittney laughed and shook her head. "Okay, now you're being an ass. She can't be at two places at once, so it makes sense that you would need to sign for the tables."

"She needs a lesson in money management. That's what she needs."

"Please tell me you didn't mansplain to her. I get that Ashley is difficult—which, by the way, she does to get a rise out of you. Even Mom has said she's stubborn. But try not to murder her. Mom needs her when she's back. She can't do it all on her own, and you aren't hanging around forever, right?"

I sighed. "She makes me so damn mad."

"You tolerated me through our teens, and I was a pain in the ass. Surely you can deal with Ashley for a few months." She narrowed her eyes, shooting me her *stop being an idiot* look.

It was cute, all five foot four and barely a hundred pounds of her trying to look intimidating. We shared our father's dark features, but my taller, bulkier build far outweighed her tiny frame.

I huffed. "Mom should have just listened when I told her she should let this whole catering thing go."

Few people understood why my mom continued to do backbreaking work when she didn't need to. But after twenty years of being controlled by her family and then spending the next twenty years dealing with the hours my dad worked— while raising my sister and me—she loved the freedom she now had to do something for herself. She had been passionate about cooking since I could remember, so it made sense to me.

"You know why she didn't, and you love her and want her to be happy, so that's why you're doing this for her. Right?"

"Yeah, yeah. I know. I wish you could cook so *you* could work with Ashley."

"Hey! I *can* cook. It just doesn't come naturally to me like it does to you. Apparently, I'm heavy-handed with the salt. But I have faith in you, Jackson. You *can* do this. Just find a way to work together."

I let out a long breath. Brittney was right. First order of business, resolve our fight from earlier. I didn't want to take the hospital event away from her, and it wasn't fair to ask her to do both.

Picking up my phone, I shot off a text.

> Me: I'll be there tomorrow to sign for the tables. Work the hospital event with me, and I'll take Saturday too.

> Ashley: Thanks.

Chapter Four

ASHLEY

"HE'S LATE. AGAIN." I bit out, grabbing another armload of stuff from the back of the van. If I wasn't here, poor Kelly would be unloading on her own. He was the one who was adamant about working this event, and now he wasn't even here.

"Maybe he hit traffic." Kelly stacked the rolling carts with the items I handed her. We usually had Miguel to help with setup and breakdown, but he was out of town this weekend, so we really could've used the extra pair of hands.

I raised my eyebrows at her, and she had the decency to blush. Traffic wasn't really a thing in our small town.

I looked up as Jackson's Aston Martin whipped into the parking lot and he pulled into a spot. Kelly sighed when he emerged from the car. Jackson was dressed in tailored black pants and a pressed white dress shirt. As usual, his top two buttons were undone while his sleeves were rolled up to his elbows. He looked like a model who'd stepped right out of *GQ* magazine. A silver chain around his neck and a sleek black watch completed the look.

"Close your mouth, Kelly. You'll catch bugs."

She rolled her eyes. "Like you weren't drooling. You may not like him, but trust me, I see the way you look at him." She gave me a wink before turning back to her task.

"Hey, princess." Jackson smirked.

"I see the watch didn't help," I said with a forced smile, nodding at his wrist.

"Help?"

"Get you here on time."

"Is that what people use them for?" Jackson's eyes widened comically as he looked between me and his watch.

"Oh my god. You're impossible." I couldn't help but chuckle. "You know what? Just help Kelly unload the van. I'll be inside." I turned and stopped almost immediately at Jackson's next words.

"Never took you for a Louboutin type of girl."

Spinning back around, I glared at him as his gaze hardened.

My shoes are none of his damn business.

"What type of girl is that? One who works hard and treats herself on occasion?" Not that I needed to explain the knock-offs. Not to this asshole.

"One who spends thousands of dollars on *shoes*."

"But it's perfectly acceptable for you to spend two hundred grand on a car?"

Kelly was frozen with a bin of utensils in her hands, swiveling her head back and forth like she was watching a tennis match.

His brows knitted together before he shook his head. He

31

mumbled something under his breath, and I spun and walked away. Officially done with him and this ludicrous conversation.

I stood in the hospital's lobby surveying the progress we'd made. It took the three of us almost an hour to get everything ready. There were two long tables on each side that held the food, and my new pub tables were scattered around where people had started to gather. Directly in front of me, the wall of floor-to-ceiling windows made the space light and airy.

I was floored when I'd arrived to find the new tables already set up. Without prompting, Jackson had put them together and driven them over here. And at some point, he'd filled the van with gas. It almost made me soften to him, but I stopped that impulse when it dawned on me that he probably didn't do it for *me.* He was here to help his mom, and as much as I couldn't stand him, I couldn't blame him for loving his mama.

I didn't have to like him, but I didn't need to be a bitch either. So made a mental note to find him and thank him later.

As if my mind summoned the sexy, swaggering devil himself, Jackson appeared in front of me a moment later and turned to stand at my side, surveying the space.

"Thank you for filling up the van and setting up the tables. I appreciate that you're taking your job seriously. I'm sure it doesn't mean anything to you, but it's important to me. I know you think it's stupid, but they look great in here." There. That wasn't so hard.

He turned slowly to face me, his mouth hanging open and his eyes wide. But in the next moment, his charming grin was plastered onto his annoyingly sexy face again.

"I agree. I thought they were going to be a pain in the ass, but the storage cart made them easy to transport and set up." His smile shot straight to my core.

Damn him and the stupid smirk that did funny things to me.

I excused myself to check in with Kelly and the two other servers who roamed the room with trays of hors d'oeuvres for the guests. Since Callahan's Classic Events was a family-owned business, we only had a few employees. For now. My goal was to help expand the size of the business and add to the types of services it provided.

Thirty minutes later, I stood off to the side, scanning the small crowd, when the hairs on the back of my neck stood up. Barry, one of the hospital board members, sidled up next to me before his uninvited hand landed on my ass. I spun to face him, and I was knocked back by the smell of whiskey on his breath.

"You ready to let me take you on that date yet?" he slurred, standing far too close.

Jesus, the event had just started and he was already three sheets to the wind.

"No, Barry. I've told you repeatedly that I'm not interested, and that isn't going to change."

"You ungrateful bitch," he hissed, reaching out to grab my arm. "And to think I'm the one who suggested you cater this event."

I pulled my arm away, attempting to take a step back. "I appreciate the opportunity. But we both know that the board wouldn't ask anyone else. Their top donors are Ed and Jackson Vargas." I swallowed, needing space from this creep sooner rather than later, and took another step back. "So—" My voice lodged in my throat when I spotted Jackson moving swiftly toward us with a murderous look on his face.

Shit, he better not make a scene.

A mix of spice and lavender hit my nose when Jackson stepped up next to me, taking up the small space with his large form. "Barry, unless you want me to tell the board I'm pulling my donation next year and why, I suggest you find someone else to harass. Or better yet, go home and sleep it off," Jackson gritted out, his rage barely controlled behind a forced smile that looked friendly but was anything but.

"Jackson, good to see you here tonight." The switch was immediate. Barry's smooth-talking corporate façade was back in place as he reached out to shake Jackson's hand. "I thought you declined the invitation."

Barry was good-looking and maybe ten years older than me, but he was a drunk and a pig under that attractive exterior, and I was sick of his unwanted advances.

Jackson looked at Barry's outstretched hand but didn't uncross his arms to accept it. "Officially, I had to decline. I'm here to help Ashley tonight." His jaw clenched twice before he continued. "Now, let's leave her be so she can do her job." Jackson took two subtle steps forward, looming over Barry, and growled his next words. "And Barry? If you ever lay hands on her again without her invitation, I won't be so nice about it. Understand?"

"We were just talking," he mumbled in Jackson's direction. "Nice to see you again, Ashley." He attempted a wan smile before walking away.

"You're welcome," Jackson muttered before I'd had a chance to thank him.

"I didn't ask you to save me," I huffed.

"I know. You never need anyone. That must get awful lonely, princess." He turned to walk away, and my instinct got the better of me, because I might not have asked, but I was relieved he had come to my aid anyway.

I grabbed his biceps, instantly wishing I hadn't. The echo of the growly voice he'd used on Barry combined with the bulge of muscle under my hand sent desire coursing through me.

"Thank you, Jackson."

He glanced at me over his shoulder and our eyes locked. I felt raw and vulnerable in that moment, but I choked it down, refusing to let that weakness rule my life again. He gave me a brief nod and walked off, giving me space to breathe again.

Chapter Five

JACKSON

I CLIMBED into the back seat of Rhett's truck as we got ready to leave for the haunted hayride. This wasn't typically my thing. But between this, the benefit a week ago, and the fact that I was now running a catering company, I wasn't sure I could define my *thing* anymore.

But it would never be hayrides. These things were excuses for guys to snuggle up with their girls, which maybe I'd be less opposed to if I had a girl.

Skipping this wasn't an option, though. Rhett and Bella had a babysitter watching Brendan tonight, and Rhett hadn't given me the choice to say no because Bella wanted to make it a group thing.

The guy was completely whipped, and yet I found myself jealous yet again. So as much as I wanted to skip it, I threw my best friend a bone and showed up. And Ashley was coming. The woman made me completely nuts most of the time, but still, I kept finding reasons to see her.

What was wrong with me?

I'd groaned when I parked in the driveway and spotted the woman who had been making my life difficult standing in jeans that might have been a second skin. I gave myself one minute to stare at her ass before I schooled my features and focused on not letting Rhett catch me checking out his sister.

Since the drive to the farm was forty-five-minutes and parking could be tight on a Saturday night, it made sense to carpool. Our buddy Dylan and the chick he was dating, plus Rhett's other sisters and Brittney would meet us there.

Seriously, what was wrong with us? We were a group of twenty-five to thirty-year-olds who had nothing better to do on Saturday night than go on a hayride? Weren't there any Oktoberfests nearby?

I rubbed a hand over the back of my neck and stole a quick glance at Ashley as she settled into Rhett's truck. Her long blond hair flowed down around her shoulders, and I couldn't help but follow it down to exactly where I shouldn't be looking.

"Bro," Rhett said.

My heart skipped a beat.

I darted my gaze to Rhett's in the rearview mirror. *Shit,* had he caught me checking out his sister? Fuck me. I was man enough to admit I'd been doing that a lot lately. Not to Rhett, but to myself.

Images of her the night I'd driven her home still haunted me six months later. She'd been wasted and carefree. Every single one of her normal inhibitions gone, and a fun, free-spirited girl I'd rarely seen had come out to play. I would give anything to see her unravel again and let down those carefully constructed walls.

I swallowed thickly. "What?"

"I was asking if you remember the name of that place we stayed in Cancun."

"Oh. Um... no, sorry. I don't. That whole week is a blur."

"I bet. Between the amount of alcohol you consumed that week and the number of women you hooked up with."

A huff of disgust came from the uptight blonde next to me, and I couldn't help but shoot her a wink.

"Dude, from what I can remember, you weren't innocent that week either."

He glanced over at Bella. "Don't believe anything he says, baby. He's just jealous of us."

I barked out a laugh. "Nah, I prefer the bachelor life."

I wasn't going to admit it, but in a way, he was right. Not because he was with Bella. But I was envious of what they had. He'd found the perfect combination with her.

Bella turned in her seat, giving me a smile. "Oh Jackson, just you wait. One day you're going to meet your match, and she'll make you eat those words. Don't you agree, Ashley?"

Ashley's mouth twitched. "Nope. But I guess there has to be someone dumb enough out there."

"Ouch. That was mean, even for you." I slapped a hand over my heart dramatically.

She rolled her eyes and angled toward the window. One step forward and two steps back with this one.

"Told you this was a bad idea," Rhett whispered to Bella. "You're never gonna get those two to get along."

"They're our best friends, so I hoped they would *eventually* try."

"Not likely," Ashley and I said in unison before a sexy little chuckle escaped her mouth.

"Well—at least you two can agree on something," Rhett said before the cab of the truck filled with silence again.

A bump and slight turn in the road caused Ashley to lean

into me, a floral smell hitting my nose. She was close enough that I could've buried my face in her hair to find out if it was coming from her shampoo or her perfume.

"Just can't get enough of me, huh?" I held her gaze for a moment before training my attention on her lips. Whatever shit she put on made them appear plump and glistening, and I struggled to tear my eyes away.

"Don't flatter yourself. It was just the sharp turn." She rolled her eyes and shifted closer to the window again.

"I really loved the crab-stuffed mushrooms you dropped off earlier this week for us to try," Bella directed at Ashley after turning in her seat to look at her.

"Really? They weren't too cheesy?" Ashley nibbled on her nail.

"Nah, they were good. You can't ever have too much cheese," Rhett chimed in.

I held back a huff. You could absolutely have too much cheese. That was the difference between someone who could taste intricate flavors in food and someone who classified food as either good or not good.

"My favorite was the bacon and cheddar cup thing," Rhett continued. "I did *not* like the one with fig."

"I liked both of them. But I love everything you make." Bella smiled and shrugged.

That wasn't really helpful. But it wasn't my place to jump in. Maybe next time, if she would be willing to accept constructive feedback, I could offer to try one of her new recipes. But maybe she used Bella and Rhett as taste testers because she liked being told what she wanted to hear.

"They're called phyllo bites, Rhett," Ashley corrected. "I plan to make some using smoked salmon and some with pancetta next."

"Rhett and Bella taste test recipes for you?" I asked and

continued when she gave me a small nod. "Would you use cream cheese with the salmon one?"

One thing I had learned was that she could talk about food for hours. Which was something we had in common.

"I don't know—I'm thinking goat cheese. It would give it more of a savory flavor. Don't you think?" She tucked her hair behind her ear before tilting her head in my direction.

"Yeah, I think you're right. That would work better texture-wise too." I nodded, imagining the combination.

Her smile grew wide, like a kid who'd been told they'd done a good job.

"This is exactly why you need to try culinary school again. I still don't understand why you haven't," Bella interjected.

Ashley's smile fell instantly.

"Again?" I couldn't help the question that escaped my mouth.

I itched to ask a million questions; I wanted to pull back all her layers and find the stuff she kept hidden away from most of the world. Maybe we were more alike than either of us knew.

Ashley crossed her arms and glared at Bella

"Sorry," Bella mumbled and quickly changed the subject, signaling that the conversation was off-limits.

By the time our whole group bought tickets and we were in line for the ride, the temperature had dropped from chilly sweater weather to outright cold. The second time Ashley squeezed her arms tighter around herself and rubbed her arms, I couldn't stay quiet any longer.

"Here," I said, taking off my lightweight North Face jacket and handing it to her. "You're freezing," I added when she raised her brows at my jacket.

She pressed her lips together in a stubborn pout, like it was a peace offering she wasn't willing to accept. I held it open for her and smirked when she eventually turned and slid one arm in. I brushed her hair off her shoulder so she could put her arm in the other sleeve and felt the shiver that ran through her body at the contact. When she faced me again and our eyes met for a beat too long, my muscles clenched and desire shot through me. And now I wanted to find out if the cold had caused her to shiver or if it had been my touch.

"Thanks. I hate being cold. I'm kicking myself for leaving my jacket in my car." Her statement and the immediate step back she took were like a knife slicing through the tension between us.

"I usually run hot, so it's all good." I shrugged. Neither one of us wanted to go there, so I didn't mind following her lead to safer territory.

Savannah mumbled under her breath before winking at me. "With that ass, you can warm me up anytime."

Savannah had absolutely no filter, and she said and did things just to get a rise out of people.

Ashley rolled her eyes at her youngest sister's crude comment. But *I* couldn't help but smile. Even though all of Rhett's sisters were attractive—not that I'd ever tell him I thought so—Savannah had always made me laugh.

"Don't encourage her," Rhett hissed in my direction with a punch to the shoulder.

"I don't think *that* one needs encouragement." I bit back a laugh when he groaned.

My sister stepped up beside me as we got ready to board the wagon.

"Have you seen the one-night stand dude again?"

Brittney nodded. "Yep. You know that new guy the owners were bringing in at work?" She cringed.

"No way." Talk about a small world. "Wait, where'd you meet him?"

"In Lake Tahoe at The Silver Lining bar. You know; the one I told you about with the dollar bills on the wall? What

41

are the chances he shows up as my new boss weeks later?" She shook her head.

"That must be really awkward." I sat down in the hay next to her, but I couldn't help but focus on Ashley as she climbed the stairs onto the wagon. "To bump into someone you casually slept with, let alone have to work with them every day." Yet another reason for me to keep my distance. The last thing we needed was to make working together even more difficult.

"Wait. Did you two finally—"

"No. Hell no." I glared at my little sister. "I told you that isn't gonna happen."

"Find a seat, miss," one of the attendants said, drawing my attention.

Ashley was eyeballing the last open spot—directly beside me—with disdain.

"I don't bite, you know. Unless you want me to," I whispered to her when she finally plopped down, causing her breath to hitch. Our proximity shouldn't have been so exciting to me, but I was smiling like an idiot all the same.

"Shut up." Ashley scooted a little closer to the end, putting a few more inches of space between us.

This should be fun.

I rested my arm behind her on the edge of the wagon. Ashley jumped when it lurched forward and grabbed a section of her hair, twirling it in her fingers.

"You scared?" I said teasingly.

"N-no."

The wagon stopped, and eerie music played louder through speakers hidden somewhere nearby. I wanted to laugh at Ashley. She was glancing in all directions, trying to prepare herself for what might happen next. I had been dreading this all day, but watching Ashley from so close while she smiled nervously made me think this evening might be fun after all.

A giant fake spider dropped suddenly from the trees

above, making half the occupants of the wagon screech, including Ashley. And since I couldn't help but tease her, I used the hand I'd rested behind her to brush against her arm; she screamed and then slapped my thigh. It took everything in me not to laugh at her. I was enjoying this *far* too much.

The next time the wagon stopped, actors dressed in costumes descended on us. Of course, they picked out the weakest links, the ones they knew would respond the best to their pestering. I always wondered how they knew. I prided myself on reading people, and even I didn't think I could do that.

One of the actors came around to the back of the wagon where we sat. Ashley inched herself away from the edge until our knees touched and I thought she was going to climb onto my lap.

I didn't hate that idea. Worse, I encouraged it when I wrapped my arm around her shoulders and pulled her into me, whispering, "Ignore them. Don't make eye contact and they'll move on."

She looked up at me with mischief in her eyes. "But what's the fun in that?"

Her fingers brushed against the side of my thigh, and my stomach tightened at her touch. She was so close, only a few inches away. I could've leaned down and pressed my lips to hers if I wanted. And *fuck*, did I want to. This fun, relaxed version of Ashley was even harder to resist than the uptight one I'd been working with for weeks.

"Hey!"

I jerked away from Ashley at the sound of her brother's voice.

"Hands to yourself over there!" Rhett glared from where he and Bella sat across from us.

I threw my hands in the air and forced a chuckle. "Don't

worry, she still hates me. I was just protecting her from the big, bad monsters."

Brittney leaned over and whispered, "Your best friend is an idiot if he can't see you two are hot for each other."

Shit, was I being obvious? Why was it so hard to stop this game I kept playing? I'd always flirted and teased her, riled her up. But now? This was different. Brittney's words hit me right in the gut. *Hot for each other.* Was Ashley as attracted to me as I was to her?

Lost in my thoughts, I gritted my teeth when she gripped my forearm. It sent a shock through my body that traveled straight to my cock. I locked eyes with her and bit back a groan at the desire swimming in those aqua orbs. She pulled her hand back suddenly, like she'd been burned, but it was her touch that had seared the skin on my forearm.

I wished I didn't want her so much. Most of the time, I thought of her as a spoiled, ungrateful brat, but there was another side to her that intrigued me. When those walls came down, it was beautiful and sexy. *She* was beautiful and sexy.

Ashley hated me, though, and she would never—at least when she was sober—allow me to touch her. But the way she taunted me as she stood in the middle of her apartment that night six months ago ran through my head.

I shook my head to keep those thoughts from clouding my judgment. It didn't matter; I wouldn't risk losing my best friend over this attraction when I knew the possibility of us was beyond unlikely. There was a bro code for a reason. Not to mention Rhett's brother Kyle would kick my ass too.

But *fuck,* when she smiled like that and let fun Ashley come out to play, I wanted to throw all those reasons out the goddamn window.

Chapter Six

ASHLEY

LIKE TWO SHIPS passing in the night, Jackson and I spent the next week on opposite schedules, just the way I had planned it. I should have been relieved, but as I drove back to the office from tonight's event, I secretly hoped he would be there prepping for tomorrow's orders. I could've gone home tonight. Could have come in early Sunday morning to get things done. But I was restless. And I had a bottle of wine stashed at the office I'd enjoy while I worked.

Miguel had left the fire hall thirty minutes before me to bring the van back and unload it. But when I pulled into my parking spot, I spotted the van, but not Miguel. He must have unloaded in record time and headed home.

I ran my fingers through my hair, homing in on Jackson's stupid Aston Martin. Damn it. But after debating whether to head home or go inside for a long moment, I finally said *to hell with it*. When I walked into the large open kitchen, I stopped dead in my tracks, a gasp sticking in my throat.

What the hell is he doing?

Jackson stood with his back to me. From my vantage point, it looked like he was cutting something. He had an earbud in his right ear, and his soulful voice sounded throughout the space, all but stopping my heart when the lyrics finally hit me.

The song by Rascal Flatts spoke of a young girl who had been diagnosed with cancer. Raw sentiment and pain vibrated through his vocals, almost like he was living through the experience he was singing about.

My own emotion bubbled up as he crooned about the girl losing her hair and her prom date showing up with a freshly shaved head. I was fixated, to put it mildly, watching this man who never seemed to be anything other than the life of a party expose himself on a deeper level.

I was intruding on a private moment; he thought he was alone. But before I could retreat to my office, the knife he was using clanged against the counter, startling the gasp I'd been holding from my lungs.

He turned, locked eyes with me for a long moment, then removed his earbuds and placed them in their case. "Sorry. Didn't hear you come in." He tossed the case on the counter with one hand and rubbed the other along the nape of his neck.

"Sorry about that." I didn't really know what to say, feeling like I invaded his privacy. "Jackson... that was beautiful."

He flinched like I stabbed him.

"It's depressing. This is more my jam." He pushed a button on his phone and "Chicken Fried" played. It was one of my favorites, and I couldn't help but join in as he plastered on a grin and belted out the lyrics. He closed the distance and grabbed my hand, bringing me toward him. His other hand landed on my hip before he led me through a spin. Some instinctive part of me knew he needed this. The pain I heard and saw when he'd faced me had been burned into my memory.

By the time the song ended, the mood was lighter and we were both smiling and a bit out of breath. The first notes of the next song rang out, but he paused his playlist only a measure or two in.

"That's better. Now, what are you doing here? Everything go okay tonight? Miguel didn't mention any issues when we unloaded the van. I figured you'd be at home soaking in a hot bath or something by now," he said, his brows knit together.

"Everything went fine. I just, uh, didn't want to go home. Thought I'd stop by and prep a few things for tomorrow."

"I had the same idea, I guess." He shrugged and waved at the ham he was dicing.

"What? No hot date on a Saturday night?"

He chuckled and shook his head before responding. "Matter of fact, I did have a date. Her name is Barbara, and she's a sweetheart, but a total control freak who wanted to make sure we weren't running her precious baby into the ground."

I laughed. Of course she did. "Since we're both here, let's see how much we can get done. Both orders are pretty big."

"Sounds good. I have the crusts for the quiches done." He picked up the knife he'd abandoned and pointed to the other side of the island where the pastries were lined up.

"I'll work on the filling if you want to continue with the add-ins."

He smiled and gestured to his phone. "Mind if I play music while we work?"

"By all means. I like to listen to music too."

We worked side by side, singing along to almost every word. As much as I tried, I couldn't keep myself from studying him every few minutes. He wore one of those skintight long-sleeve athletic shirts tucked into the waistband of gray sweatpants, showcasing how defined his muscles were, the tattoos on both forearms visible below the sleeves he had pushed to his elbows.

Bella and I made fun of romance novels that always portrayed men in gray sweatpants as sexy as fuck. Neither of us had ever understood the hype. I had two brothers, so maybe I was used to it. But seeing Jackson in them gave me a better understanding. They hugged him in all the right places. His singing added to his appeal—that deep, sultry voice caused shivers to run up my spine.

By the time the quiches were prepped, that hot bath and a glass of wine sounded real good.

"Damn, now I understand why Mom has back issues." Jackson had his hands on his lower back and was arching back.

"Not easy work, is it?" I smirked, knowing I was poking the bear.

"Never said it was." His tone held a bite to it.

For once, I didn't want to fight with him. Maybe I was just too damn tired.

I glanced around the kitchen and sighed. "I guess we better work on cleaning this mess up."

He raised his gaze back to mine and held it for what felt like forever. It was unnerving, like he was looking for answers in my expression.

He finally looked away and said, "I can clean up if you want to head home. You must be dead on your feet."

His offer was tempting, but leaving the mess for him didn't sit right.

"Thank you, but I can stay. We'll get it done quicker if we

work together, and then we can go to bed." I froze at the possible implication of what I'd said.

He whipped his head back up with one eyebrow raised.

"Uh, I mean our own separate beds. You go home to your bed, and I'll go home to mine." I wished he would stop looking at me like that. "Ugh, never mind. You know what I meant." I rolled my eyes and turned away from him.

He chuckled behind me, and then music blared from his phone again. I bit back a grin when he started dramatically singing and dancing around to "T-shirt" by Thomas Rhett. Going home with him and waking up in his T-shirt wouldn't be that bad, would it?

Shit, I needed to stop going there. Remind myself of all the reasons I hated him. Not that I needed to like a man to want to fuck him, right? But hooking up with a coworker was never a good idea.

After we'd finished cleaning the kitchen, I kicked off my flats, grabbed a bottle of water, and hoisted myself up onto the counter to give my feet a break. In the next moment, my resolve to keep things strictly friendly, or not so friendly, was a lost cause. When his eyes, smoldering with lust, traveled the length of my body, a hot wave of desire coursed through me. Maybe he was an asshole, but that didn't stop my body from responding to the way he examined me like he was imagining me naked and spread out for him.

I wanted—no, needed—to feel his hands on me. And I didn't give a damn about the consequences.

Chapter Seven

I spun away from the cabinet I'd just put the mixing bowls in to find Ashley sitting on the stainless-steel counter-top, sipping on a bottle of water. Not sure when she discarded her shoes, but my eyes traveled from her bare feet up to the short black skirt that rode high on her thighs. Her top had caught my eye one too many times tonight, but I absolutely couldn't go there. She was my best friend's little sister, I reminded myself for the millionth time. But the sheer light-gray blouse with the first three buttons undone covering a tight, low-cut tank had me gaping at her chest once again.

My gaze traveled farther up as she brought the water bottle to her mouth, and I imagined what else she could wrap her lips around. Those pretty blues regarded me for a moment before she smiled and leaned back slightly, pushing her gorgeous tits up and out.

"Like what you see?" she asked as she licked her lips.

Fuck me.

Was that even a legitimate question? Of course I liked what I saw. She was fucking stunning, and my dick agreed. I turned away from her to adjust myself and placed one hand on the cabinet in front of me, bowing my head and trying to gain some control over my fucked-up desire.

"You know I do."

I expected a snarky reply, but the silence that lingered in the air surprised me. Glancing over my shoulder, I locked eyes with a darker shade of blue, swimming with desire. Her tongue traced along her bottom lip as she ever so slowly undid the buttons of her sheer top.

What was she doing? Teasing me or—*fuck*, there went the last button, and now her breasts were practically on display where they were barely restrained by her tiny tank. I took two cautious steps toward her, itching to reach out and grab a handful of each of those perfect mounds. She sucked in a sharp breath when she gave me a once-over, noticing my out-of-control cock. When our eyes met again, hers darkened once more.

Fuck it.

I closed the distance between us and grabbed her by the hips, yanking her to the edge of the counter. She uncrossed her legs, and I wedged myself between them. As she wrapped them around my waist, I crushed my mouth against hers. The urgency with which she responded was more intense than anything I'd ever experienced. She didn't just take what I was giving; she gave it right back. Her hands were in my hair, tugging me closer. She bit my lower lip, then sucked it into her mouth. I groaned, pushing my way into her mouth and deepening the kiss.

"Fuck, I knew this would be good," I mumbled, trailing kisses around to her ear. "I've wanted to do this since that night you were drunk and wanted me to fuck you," I said as I continued my way down her neck.

She froze at my admission.

God dammit.

Her hands landed on my shoulders, and she pushed me away while I took a deep breath to regain my composure.

"What did you say?"

Maybe I could backtrack. "I've wanted to do this since that night I drove you home from the bar." I rubbed the back of my neck as she leveled me with a look so powerful it almost took me down right there.

"That is *not* exactly what you said." Her glare said she wasn't buying my bullshit. "I did not want you to fuck me that night."

"Oh, princess. Trust me, you did. Just like you do right now." I smirked as I took in her still-rapid breathing and the hard nipples showing through her tank. "You stripped out of your shirt and bra and danced around, telling me in detail exactly how hard and fast you wanted it."

"I did not!"

I took a deep breath and held it, letting my eyes close for a long moment. "Do you always have to argue?"

"When you're wrong, yes."

I pinned her with my stare. "You have a small butterfly tattoo on the side of your left tit."

"You could have seen that any time we were out on the boats."

"Nope. I am very observant when it comes to your tits. You only wear those bikini tops that look like bras, which cover the whole tattoo. I never knew it was there until that night." I chuckled.

Her eyes were wide, and she opened and closed her

mouth, but no words came out. I loved that sometimes I rendered her speechless. It was few and far between.

"This isn't funny," she hissed.

"It's hilarious. I've wondered for years how to shut you up. Apparently, telling you I saw you half naked did the trick."

She reached out and slapped my chest. "I can't believe I threw myself at you. *And* you turned me down. And I don't even remember any of it."

I placed my hands on either side of her on the counter and tipped forward so my face was inches from hers. "Don't mistake me leaving that night as anything other than wanting to do the right thing. The memory of you topless is one I recall quite frequently." I grinned as her mouth formed a perfect *O* at my implication.

"Your rendition of "Drunk Girl" makes even more sense now." She looked away, her cheeks going pink.

I sang that song in front of all of our friends one night this past summer. Only Ashley and I knew the meaning behind it. At least that's what I thought. But apparently, she remembered very little about that night back in April. Her inhibition had been so unlike her, and I was still curious about why she took it that far.

I tilted her chin with my finger. "And I meant every word of it. I know you've always thought of me as an asshole, and most of the time I am. But that's something I'd never do. I want you, Ashley. I wanted you that night. But not like that." I shook my head and stepped back. What the fuck was I saying? I may have wanted her, but I couldn't have her. "I should probably go before we do something we'll regret."

"Probably." She smirked like she wouldn't mind the consequences.

I groaned, turning away from her. I grabbed my stuff and headed toward the exit. "I'll be in at eight," I called over my shoulder.

Driving toward home, I replayed the night. The memory of her lips on mine and her fingers in my hair had my cock stirring all over again.

I needed to get a grip.

It had been months since I'd gotten laid; maybe that was my issue. But after a long string of *flavors of the week* who expected me to spend my money on them, the pull for another casual hookup was unappealing. Although the girl I dated back in May hadn't been casual. I tried to make it more, but I just couldn't. We had nothing in common, and opening up to her proved to be a struggle.

The only woman I could imagine in my bed was the one I'd just walked away from.

Rhett's gonna kick my ass.

My phone lit up where it was secured on the dash. Ashley's name flashed across the screen, and I contemplated not answering. I had just left her, for god's sake, and I was trying to do the right thing here. But I hit the answer button on the steering wheel anyway.

"Jackson?" she asked, panic laced through her voice.

"Hey, everything okay?"

"Uh, well, not really. I need some help."

The line disconnected, and I cursed. I tried calling back twice, and her voice mail picked up both times. What the hell?

I turned the car around and headed back to her, hoping she was still there. I let out a relieved breath when I spotted her car still in its spot. But when I walked into the kitchen and saw broken glass and blood on the floor, my heart stopped.

"Ash?"

"Here." A hand popped up from the other side of the island.

I stepped over the glass and crouched next to her. "What the fuck happened?"

"I cut my hand." She looked at her right hand wrapped in a towel.

"No shit, I gathered that. How?" I reached for her hand, and after a moment of reluctance, she let me take it. "It might need stitches," I said after uncovering the cut and looking at it.

"Absolutely not. It'll be fine. Just help me clean it and wrap it. It looks worse than it is."

"Maybe, but—"

"Jackson Vargas. I am not going to the ER. If my family or your mom hear that I cut my hand and needed stitches, they'll be like bees on honey. Remember how annoyed you got about the meal train? My family, your family, the whole goddamn town will want to help, and neither of us can handle that. So let's try to avoid that, agreed?"

I laughed; she was right. But still. "If we can't stop the bleeding, then you need to go, okay?"

"Yes, of course."

"Wait here. Let me grab the first aid kit." When I returned, she was standing at the sink. "I told you to wait, stubborn woman." I shook my head when she shrugged.

After helping her clean it, I took a better look. She was right. It wasn't as bad as I'd initially thought. I placed a few Steri-Strips along the cut, covered it with a piece of gauze, and wrapped it in a self-adhesive bandage. "There, that should do it."

"Thank you." She waved at the glass on the floor. "I should get that cleaned up now."

"I'll do it."

"It's just a cut. I'm not helpless. Let me go grab the dustpan and broom." She rolled her eyes and disappeared in the direction of the supply closet.

"You ready to tell me what happened now? And why your phone kept going to voice mail when I called you back?" I asked once we had the mess cleaned up.

55

"I thought it was pretty self-explanatory." She tilted her head and her brow furrowed. "I dropped a wineglass, and I guess I put my hand on a piece of glass when I knelt to clean it up. Then my phone died. It hasn't been holding a charge for long lately. I probably need a new one, but I really don't want to deal with the hassle."

"Yeah, you should probably take care of that. What if you get stuck in a more serious situation and have no way to call for help?"

"Thanks for the lecture. I appreciate it." She pushed past me in a tizzy.

One step forward, two steps back.

"Ash, wait." I came up behind her and ran my hand down her arm, grinning when her breath hitched. "Didn't mean to lecture. Why don't you take tomorrow off? I'll finish and deliver the orders."

"I can't. I have an appointment in the city tomorrow anyway." She slipped on her shoes and grabbed her keys from the counter.

"So do I. Let's ride together." The city was only an hour's drive, but it wouldn't be a comfortable one with an injured dominant hand.

"I can drive myself, Jackson. I appreciate your help tonight, but really, I'm fine."

"I know. But the cut will heal faster if you take it easy. Besides, I want to try these cupcakes you and my mom keep raving about."

She put her uninjured hand on her hip. "How do you know I have an appointment with the bakery?"

"It's on our shared calendar." I shrugged.

She looked away and sighed, letting her shoulders slump. "Fine. I'll meet you here at eight. We can finish the orders, drop them off, and make the drive to Asheville together."

We walked to our cars after locking up the building. I

didn't want to push my luck, but I had to offer. "Want me to give you a ride home?"

Her glare said it all. "No, I literally live eight minutes away. I'll be fine."

"I figured," I mumbled before she climbed into the driver's seat and drove off.

I braced my hand on the top of the car as I second-guessed what the hell I was doing. Taking her with me tomorrow? Showing her a part of my life that only a handful of people knew about? Introducing her to Sophia?

Had I gone and lost my mind, or was I just thinking with the wrong head?

Chapter Eight

ASHLEY

I STARED at the clothes hanging in my closet. The question floating through my mind had nothing to do with being clueless about where I was going. Although I should be wondering what kind of meeting Jackson had, I was instead debating what outfit would give me the best chance at having Jackson's lips on mine. I couldn't stop reliving the way his fingers dug into my sides and pulled me toward him. With my fingers to my lips, I sank into the memory of the no-holds-barred way he crushed his mouth to mine.

I yanked the blue sweater dress off the hanger and paired it with black boots that ended past my knees, hoping Jackson wouldn't be able to resist. Go big or go home, right? I pinned back a few pieces of hair and let the rest flow down around my shoulders.

My hand was a little sore today, but overall, it was fine. I could have driven myself to Asheville. My normal MO would be to call and say I was fine, and I'd take care of myself. But I wanted to see Jackson. And I wanted Jackson to see me.

Touch me.

Almost giddy, I arrived at the office, ready to spend the day with the guy who, until recently, I couldn't stand. I shook my head at the massive shift that had already taken place. Strike that. It wasn't that massive. I wasn't sure I liked Jackson. But boy was I tired of pretending I didn't want him.

"Nice boots." The way Jackson's heated gaze roamed over my body and the corner of his mouth tipped up into a devilish grin were concrete evidence that I'd made the right decision when I'd chosen the dress and boots.

Ridiculously, I wanted him to touch me again. To light my skin on fire like he did last night.

"Thanks. What can I do? I guess I can't chop."

Jackson turned back to his task of cutting up fresh fruit as I waited for his direction. Which I hated. I wasn't good at following other people's lead.

Even though Barbara was technically my boss, we'd always worked side by side. I never felt like I had to answer to someone, which was one of many reasons I loved my job. Maybe it was why she and I worked so well together. We both understood what it was like to be under someone's thumb, to want something for our lives that hadn't quite worked out the way we'd hoped.

Barbara no longer had much to do with her parents. They were controlling and hadn't approved of her relationship with Jackson's dad until he got a high-paying job on Wall Street.

But after Ed's heart attack, when he moved them all to Half Moon Lake for a slower pace of life, they became disapproving once again.

That's where she and I differed. I was lucky to have the family I did.

However, I understood being controlled and manipulated. It took me too long to see the writing on the wall with my ex, Paul. The endless cycles were exhausting. He'd tell me how much he loved me and how he wanted to marry me, and then how sorry he was when he verbally lashed out at me anytime I questioned aspects of our relationship. He rarely brought me around his family and always had an excuse for why we should wait to get engaged or married. I was so in love with him, or so I thought. Looking back, I know now it was the idea of what he offered—a future I thought I wanted, one he'd fabricated from the beginning—that I was too blind to see what I deserved.

But maybe everything worked out like it was supposed to. Maybe I was meant to come home after college and help Barbara run her business.

"I can probably cook the bacon and sausages," I said, shaking myself out of my runaway thoughts and moving toward the fridge.

"Already done."

I froze, huffing and feeling useless. Like Rhett, I wasn't good at expressing emotions. I preferred to show people that I cared by doing things for them. So feeling helpless drained me. That was what made it so easy for Paul to manipulate me. He used my need to please to drag me along, my efforts never good enough.

"But they'll need to be reheated with the quiches before we leave." He used the knife he was holding to point toward the pastry boxes laid out on the stainless-steel countertop. "Maybe you could put together the container of mixed pastries?"

I bit the inside of my cheek as I dissected his words, watching the muscles in his back work as he continued to cut.

What other hidden talents did he keep locked away under all those muscles and tattoos? I bet he would be an attentive lover—the way he seemed to take in every minute detail, and how focused he was in every task. What would it be like to let him explore my body with his tongue as I writhed in pleasure?

"Ash?"

Heat trailed up my neck and into my face as I shook myself from my daydream.

"Okay—I can do that." I quickly turned, hoping he didn't know where my thoughts had gone.

After I put the pastries together, we reheated the bacon, sausages, and quiches before putting them in aluminum containers.

"How's your hand?" he asked once we were in his car, driving toward the church to drop off the first order.

"It's good. Just a little sore." I twirled a piece of hair around my finger before brushing it over my shoulder. "What kind of appointment do you have in the city today?"

His Adam's apple bobbed as he swallowed. "Yeah, I wanted to talk about that."

His tone was ominous, and if it was something we needed to talk about, it couldn't be good.

"Why do I think I shouldn't have agreed to this? But go on, I'm listening."

"You don't mind singing in front of people, right? I know you sing at church sometimes."

"Not really. I was in musicals in high school too. I enjoy it."

A clipped "good" was his response.

Before I could ask him to elaborate, we pulled up in front of the church.

"Wait here. I can run the order in," he said as he opened his door.

"I can help."

"Nah, if you come in, we'll never leave. Only people you can't be short or rude to are the church ladies."

I scoffed. "I'm not rude."

"So you never said someone would have to be stupid to date me?"

I winced. Because yup, I'd totally said that. I wished I could control my mouth better sometimes.

"Fine, you're right." I scrunched up my nose at the admission.

"Did it hurt to say that or something?"

"Oh, shut up and deliver the order."

The victorious grin he wore as he climbed out of the car had me shaking my head and chuckling.

He was right. It only took him minutes to drop off the order with the ladies at church, and then we were making our way toward our second destination.

The farther up the mountain we went, the tighter Jackson's grip on the steering wheel got.

I watched him for several long minutes before it dawned on me. "This is the road you had your accident on."

His eyes darted in my direction, his brows raised, but he didn't turn away from the road. That was a stupid thing to ask.

"It still makes you nervous?"

Oh my god, Ashley. Just stop talking.

His nostrils flared and he huffed out a hard breath. "Yeah. It's worse when I'm a passenger, but I don't like driving on it either."

I opened my mouth to ask another dumb question, but he cut me off.

"It's also my least favorite subject, so can we move on?"

I nodded, and a very silent ten minutes later, we were on our way to Asheville.

"We never finished our earlier conversation about singing in front of people."

He grabbed the back of his neck and glanced in the rearview before switching lanes.

"I visit the children's hospital in Asheville once a month. I sing to the kids while I'm there."

"Seriously?"

"Will you ever stop thinking of me as a horrible person?" He huffed, and his jaw clenched.

I didn't have a clue where to start with that. *Maybe* I had pegged him all wrong. My judgment of him when he took over for his mom had been harsh. I saw that now. I assumed he would be lazy, when in fact, he'd worked hard and had done all he could to help.

Shame swamped me for assuming the worse. However, every time I'd seen him over the last five years, he'd had a new girl hanging on him and had been drinking and goofing off with his buddies. Or teasing me like we were teenagers again. Not to mention Barbara talked about how much he traveled. It wasn't that I thought he was a horrible person, just immature. Like he refused to grow up.

"I think it's great, Jackson." I chewed the inside of my cheek. "How did you get started with that?" Maybe there was more to him than he let people see.

"My friend Bill and his wife Dani have a foster child who's been in and out of that hospital over the last three years."

When he didn't elaborate, I wanted to ask more, but I didn't want to push.

"I'd love to tag along if you're okay with it."

He glanced at me sideways, one eyebrow slightly raised. "You sure? You don't have to."

"I said yes. Now what the hell are we singing? Kid-friendly songs, I hope? I'm not sure parents would appreciate you singing about hooking up with a girl and seeing her in your T-shirt." I held back a grin, thinking about him singing that Thomas Rhett song last night.

He rolled his eyes. "Always with the dramatics. And yes, kid-friendly songs. I have a handful picked out. Since Halloween is tomorrow, we'll go with a few of those favorites. And I always do a few hits and a Taylor Swift song for the older kids."

We talked for the next thirty minutes about what songs he could play and which songs I could sing until we came up with a selection that would work.

"So what's the deal with the bakery?" he asked after silence settled between us again.

"Bianca's great. She makes kick-ass desserts. We've been using her since your mom's back issues started. I try to make it out here once a month to go over specialty orders and taste test her new creations. She does a lot of seasonal desserts, and she changes things up often. I'm really excited to try her pumpkin cheesecake bites." I hadn't been out here since we finalized Bella's wedding cake in early September. It hit me how busy we had been lately, and I was excited at the thought that expanding this business was actually coming to fruition.

The bakery was our first stop since my appointment with Bianca was at noon. She had quite a bit for us to sample, and we agreed on adding the pumpkin cheesecake bites and caramel apple turnovers to our menu for November. Plus the chocolate cranberry mini cakes for December, because *yum.*

I was on cloud nine when we walked outside. We had exceeded our minimum order for our contract five months in a row now, and Bianca had asked if we would consider increasing our monthly minimum to get more of a discount. It felt like we had been busier lately, but this was the proof I needed.

"Hey." Jackson wrapped a hand around my upper arm, pulling me to a stop.

I turned to face him, my mind still racing. "Yeah?"

"You know we're not gonna increase the contract yet, right?"

Being that Jackson's family owned the business, I didn't have the final say in the matter, but damn. I'd worked my ass off these last five years, and it just made sense.

"Why the hell not?" I demanded as I crossed my arms. This was why I couldn't stand him most of the time. His *I know best* attitude reminded me of my ex and grated on my nerves. Why would we pay higher prices when our sales increased consistently?

"We can't base this decision off the last five months, and you know it. Summer and fall are our busiest seasons, and you've had Bella's engagement party, bridal shower, and wedding. That won't always be the case." He mimicked my stance and crossed his arms.

"How do you know that? Bella is already planning an adoption party, of all things. At the rate she's going, Bella alone will keep us in business."

"God help Rhett," he mumbled. "But it's fucking stupid to depend on *that*."

"Fine, whatever. I should've known you wouldn't understand." I pivoted and threw open the car door, making sure to slam it behind me. Once I'd had time to think about it, I probably would have come to the same conclusion, but he just had to go rain on my parade before I could even celebrate the small win.

He stood there on the sidewalk, arms crossed and jaw clenched. Good. I hoped he was as pissed off as I was.

When he finally climbed into the car, we made our way through downtown traffic in silence while I stewed in my thoughts.

Jackson turned to me once he parked at the hospital

fifteen minutes later and asked, "Do you still want to do this? It's fine if you've changed your mind."

I tucked a strand of hair behind one ear, thinking over his question. He was giving me an out, and he was the biggest ass I knew, but part of me still wanted to be involved.

"I'm good," I said, giving him a brief nod and a forced smile.

He stared at me for an uncomfortably long time before shaking his head. "You drive me insane."

"Trust me, the feeling's mutual."

He barked out a laugh and climbed out of the car. I followed until we were in a large common area. The back of the room was set up with tables and chairs and several shelves that held books and games. Jackson grabbed two chairs and positioned them next to each other before turning to greet a nurse who entered the room. Her colorful puppy dog scrubs were as bright as her smile.

"There's our favorite singer. We've missed you around here." I gritted my teeth when she wrapped her arms around his neck and hugged him in a way that looked too familiar. She pulled back, but her hands stayed on his biceps for another moment. "Your girl has been asking for you all day. I know you talked yesterday, but she has not been able to control her excitement."

Jackson's eyes darted away, and his hand came up, brushing against the back of his head. "It's killed me that I haven't been able to visit with her as much this time."

"I know. She understands, though. And, of course, she has all those books to keep her busy." The nurse smiled before glancing over her shoulder, watching the kids pile into the room, most with parents. "I better get back to my rounds. Stop by and see me before you visit Sophia."

I swallowed, my mouth feeling dry. I had so many questions. His girl? This time? Who was Sophia?

He gave her a nod, then she turned and scurried out of the room.

Before I could ask any of the questions whirring around in my head, a little voice spoke up. "Hi, Mr. Jackson."

"Hey, buddy. How you doing?" Jackson ruffled the child's hair.

"I beat your Mario Kart score last week." The little boy sent Jackson a toothy smile.

"Aw, man. Looks like I'll have to practice some more," Jackson teased.

This side of Jackson was something I'd never known existed. He didn't just come here to sing every now and again. He knew these people, these kids.

"Is that your *girlfriend*, Mr. Jackson?" Another little voice piped up from the back and all the kids giggled.

More like the bane of his existence.

To be honest, I wasn't sure *what* I'd expected when we got here. But this lively bunch with smiles on their faces was not it.

"No. She's a good friend of mine, and we work together in Half Moon Lake. She came along today to meet you all and sing with me. What do you say? Is that okay?"

The small crowd that had gathered toward the front of the room, seated on couches and beanbag chairs, erupted approvingly. I gave them all a big smile in return.

Jackson and I went through our lineup, singing the songs we'd talked about in the car. I tried to keep it together through "The Duck Song," a silly kids' song about a duck asking a guy selling lemonade for grapes. When I couldn't hold back my laughter, Jackson just shook his head at me and continued on, but it wasn't long before the whole room was laughing.

I had fun singing "Mean" by Taylor Swift. But then my heart did some weird pinching thing toward the end of "Possibilities" by Darius Rucker when the room joined in on one of the choruses that spoke of the hope, strength, love, and laughter you get from the people in your life who love you.

We ended our time with "Monster Mash," which is never *not* a hit with kids. I stood up in front of the room full of kids and went through the moves of the accompanying dance before Jackson joined in with his guitar. With the way these kids were excitedly dancing along with me, I'd almost forgotten that we were in a hospital and each of these kids was fighting a battle for their health. Jackson's smile of approval was aimed at me when I peeked in his direction, and it sent heat creeping up my neck.

When the dance was over, the kids all waved, telling us how much fun they had, before piling out of the room. A few asked if I could come back, and I meant it when I told them I'd love to.

"You really gonna come back with me sometime?" Jackson asked.

"Yes, I really want to. That was so... I don't know. Fun sounds insensitive, but I loved watching their reactions to all the songs. All that innocent, carefree excitement." I hadn't had that much fun in a long time, and their enthusiasm was contagious.

"Yeah, I get it. Come on, there's someone I'd like you to meet." Jackson grabbed my hand and pulled me out of the room before I could respond.

Chapter Nine

JACKSON

I LEANED on the counter of the nurses' station, waiting patiently for Natasha to finish the conversation she was engrossed in. The puppy dog scrubs she was wearing today were loud even for her, but she always said that she picked ones that guaranteed smiles from the kids.

Ashley stood beside me quietly. What did she think about all this? And since when did I care so much about her opinion?

"Hey," Natasha said as she approached us. "You ready to go see Sophia?"

"Yep, we're ready. Any update on when she'll be released? Are Bill and Dani here?"

"She's going home today. And no, they aren't here yet," Natasha said before turning to Ashley with a more serious expression. "Jackson knows the deal already, but make sure to wash your hands and mask up before you go in. Sophia is immunocompromised."

"Okay," Ashley said before nodding and glancing at me with wide eyes.

I could see the questions she was dying to ask, but they'd have to wait.

"Thanks, Natasha." I shifted on my feet when she raised one eyebrow and crossed her arms. I'd never brought a girl with me who wasn't my sister, and I couldn't tell whether she approved or wanted to ask what the fuck I was thinking. Either way, she didn't seem inclined to ask me in front of Ashley.

Once we were a few steps away from the nurses, Ashley whispered, "Did you two used to date or something? I don't think she likes me very much."

"She's very protective of her patients. Don't take it personally. When I started coming here to volunteer a few years ago, she hated me. Thought I was some rich guy looking to make myself feel better." I shrugged, because at the time, she wasn't that far off base. "She eventually came around. But to answer your original question, no, I haven't dated any of the staff and don't plan to."

We stopped outside of Sophia's room, washed our hands, and donned surgical masks.

"Jackson, you made it!" Sophia cheered when we stepped into the room. Her curly dark-blond hair fell down around her shoulders, with the top of her head covered with one of her scarves.

More than a year ago, we'd spoken of the possible hair loss. She wasn't ready to shave it. She loved her long hair, and she was less likely to lose it with this kind of treatment than with many others. She'd decided to go with head caps and scarves to hide any thinning or bald spots, leaving shaving as a last resort.

Somewhere along the way, the head pieces began feeling like a part of her, and she'd decided she liked wearing them and would continue to do so sometimes.

"Of course I did. You really think I would miss seeing you before you went home?"

"I finished reading it!" Her bright smile was like a punch to the gut. I wished she could always smile like that. She had beaten cancer. She should be enjoying life again. But her little body had other plans. Her immune system was struggling, but the doctors were confident that this was just timing and that by the end of cold and flu season, she'd be able to fight off common illnesses.

"I knew you would. So now we're moving on to *Harry Potter and the Prisoner of Azkaban*?"

"Yep, started it this morning." Sophia's face lit up as her gaze moved over to Ashley. "Is this Ashley? You're right. She's pretty. And her hair is long like mine."

I ran my hand over my head and smirked. One of the reasons I loved spending time with these kids, especially Sophia, was because of how honest they were. I'd spent a day with her during one of her shorter stays just before Rhett's wedding. They had run some tests to make sure the cancer hadn't come back since it was the third time she had been sick recently. She'd peppered me with questions about the wedding and Ashley when I mentioned I had to help clean up and break down everything after the reception. I was not going to tell a ten-year-old girl that I thought Ashley was hot, so instead I said *yes, I think she's pretty and very nice*.

"It is. And yup, she's very pretty and has long, beautiful hair, just like you."

Ashley stepped forward with wide eyes, like she was surprised by my admission. But she had to know; I'd done a terrible job hiding my attraction to her.

"Do you like *Harry Potter* too?" Sophia directed at Ashley.

Books were something Sophia and I had first bonded over. We both loved fantasy the most. She had been reading *Percy Jackson* in the back of the common room during one of my first visits.

"I've seen a few of the movies, but I've never read the books." Ashley smiled as she picked up the paperback that sat on the side table. "And Jackson's right—You *do* have beautiful hair, and I love your headscarf. Do you get them online or from a store?"

"Jackson ordered me a bunch after I decided I didn't want to shave it." Sophia shrugged like it wasn't a big deal, but I knew better. I was one of the few people who had accepted her decision. "Do you like to color?" Sophia gestured to the colored pencils and coloring book on the rolling table positioned across her bed.

"I do." Ashley sat on the edge of the bed on the other side of the table and picked up a purple pencil. "You're really good at this." Ashley nodded to Sophia's page after a few minutes of coloring.

"Thanks, you are too. What happened to your hand?" Sophia asked, seeing her right hand bandaged.

"Oh. I cut myself. But it's fine now." Ashley stole a glance over her shoulder to where I sat in a chair at the foot of the bed. "Jackson came and helped me."

"He's great, isn't he? He loves helping people."

"He's pretty okay. But sometimes I don't like when he teases me."

Sophia's eyes got huge, and she looked at me and then back at Ashley. "My foster mom says boys tease girls because they like them."

I bowed my head and rubbed my hand along the back of my neck, stifling a chuckle, while Ashley laughed freely.

Over the next hour, Sophia asked rapid-fire questions about our catering events. Ashley told her stories about crazy things that had happened to her over the years, including the time someone accidentally fell into a pool.

After the third time Sophia glanced at the clock on the wall and frowned, I tilted my head and asked, "What time are Dani and Bill supposed to pick you up?"

Sophia looked away.

Shit. You've got to be kidding me.

I should have checked in with them this morning. They've had their hands full lately. Not only were they caring for Sophia, but they had a troubled teenager in their care, as well as two other foster children.

"This morning," she finally muttered. "But they got a call for another foster placement and had to get her settled. They promised they'd be here by four."

"I'm going to step out and call them. See if there's anything I can do."

"Don't. It's fine. I can wait." She shrugged.

Her maturity blew me away each and every time I saw her. "You know, most ten-year-olds wouldn't be so understanding."

"Good thing I'm not most ten-year-olds. And I'm gonna be eleven soon."

I smiled. She loved to remind me of that, even though her birthday was four months away.

"Can you believe how everything turned out with the diary?" I picked up the book she had just finished and skimmed through the pages.

"Or the girls' bathroom?" She clapped her hands in front of her as she bounced on the hospital bed. "Totally didn't see that coming!"

A few minutes later, Dani walked in. To say she looked overwhelmed was an understatement. Bill and Dani were trying their best to help in a broken system, and I admired that. In fact, because of them, I'd decided that I wanted to make a difference too. Maybe adopt at some point. That was if I could ever get through their bullshit red tape and hoops.

I had so much to offer. So much I wanted to give, but the powers that be refused to give me a chance. I ground my teeth together at the reminder, trying not to show my frustration, especially in front of Sophia.

Ashley and I said our goodbyes, and I promised to talk to Sophia soon.

Dani shook her head when I asked if they needed anything. "I don't think so, Jackson. But I don't know. Things have been crazy lately. Maybe come by soon and shoot some hoops with Adam. He seems to connect with you. Maybe you can get him to open up a bit. He thinks Bill and I are old and don't understand him." She sighed.

"He's sixteen, and he's been through some major life changes. I can relate, even though the circumstances aren't the same."

"I know. Let us know. You haven't been by for dinner in a while. Have you heard any more about your application?"

"Nope. My lawyer hasn't been too hopeful recently either." I locked my jaw. The whole situation was fucked up.

"That's a shame." She blew out a long breath.

Once the door closed behind us and we were striding down the hall, I let the smile fall from my face.

"What application was Dani talking about?" Ashley asked once we were in the elevator.

My spine stiffened. Did I want to tell her about this? *Again*? We'd had this conversation before. But this time, we were both sober.

"Adoption. I've been working with a lawyer in hopes that I can adopt Sophia. They've been giving my attorney the runaround. He thinks I don't look acceptable on paper."

When the elevator doors opened to the parking garage, I

stomped out and headed straight for my car with Ashley hot on my heels.

Once we were in the car, Ashley turned to me. "You want to adopt that little girl? Really?"

"Yeah. Are you hungry? Let's get some food, then I can fill you in on the last six months. I've already told you some of it, but it doesn't look like you remember."

Her eyebrows shot up, and she shook her head. "What are you talking about?"

"The night I drove you home from the bar... You asked why I was drinking by myself."

"Oh." She cringed. "That entire night is fuzzy." She paused, and a blush rose on her cheeks. "Even more than I realized."

Images of her dancing around her apartment flashed through my head. My hands tightened on the wheel.

"It's fine. So, food? Anything you'd prefer?"

She shook her head slightly and then stopped. "Actually, there's an amazing little French bistro not far from here."

"That place is great." I started the car and maneuvered it out onto the busy city street.

Was I really going to open up to Ashley? Sometimes things between us were so easy, like we'd been friends for years. And other times we wanted to kill each other. But something told me that despite our tumultuous interactions over the years, I could trust her with this.

Ashley

THIS FELT STRANGE. I sat across from Jackson in this quaint little bistro, rendered immobile by his unrelenting laser focus. The restaurant had been my suggestion, but now I felt out of place surrounded by all the couples occupying the nearby tables. I glanced around at the people in the restaurant as I wrung the napkin in my hands before laying it across my lap.

"Ashley?" Jackson said, his eyes burning into me. The constant, intense scrutiny made me squirm once again. I was usually the observant one, noting what was needed and just doing it. Having that type of careful consideration aimed at me now was throwing me off. "The cheese board for a starter?"

He'd asked once already, but I was nervous. It was all so much easier when I hated him—before he'd kissed me and lit a flame inside me. Before I'd met Sophia and glimpsed the depths of the compassion and generosity Jackson hid behind his playboy façade.

"Um. Sure."

He was suggesting my favorite item on the menu, and I didn't know how to process the way it made me feel. Just like in the car when he turned my seat warmer on before I even asked.

Once we ordered, he cleared his throat, but I couldn't look at him. I was afraid of what I'd see in his eyes. What he'd see written all over my face. With no menu to hide behind, I twirled my hair around one finger while he scrutinized me with a burning intensity before he leaned back and crossed his arms.

I couldn't stand it. Silence had never been my strong suit, and it wasn't Jackson's either, but the tension between us told me we were inching into new territory.

"What happened back in April that led you to the bar that night?"

His lips curved into a cocky grin before he leaned forward, and his deep voice sent a shiver through my body. "Look at that. The princess talks."

"I mean, we can just sit in silence if you want." I shrugged and tried to smooth my expression into one of apathy. I was ready to call his bluff if I needed to.

"You closed off again. Care to enlighten me as to what I did to piss you off between when we left the hospital and now?"

"I'm not pissed off. It's just—I'm not used to your... intensity. Or rather, I'm not used to it being directed toward me." I tilted my head, taking in the way his eyes widened ever so slightly at my admission. "Just be lucky I no longer want to smother you with a pillow. Now talk. I don't do silence, remember?"

He rested his forearms on the table, his voice deep and low. "Are you chatty in bed too, princess?"

I tipped forward so our faces were inches apart. "You'd love to find out, wouldn't you?"

A smirk played on his lips, and my breath caught when his attention shifted to my lips for a beat before lifting. His exhales danced on my lips as he continued to study me. An inner turmoil swam in his eyes for a moment before desire won out. He moved in—

"Sir?"

We both startled, pulling back. Jackson nodded to his glass, but the clench of his jaw said he wasn't any happier with the interruption than I was.

We thanked the waiter after he poured the wine we'd ordered.

A moment later, Jackson finally spoke. "Bill and Dani were having a rough time. Sophia was at the tail end of her treatments. Lots of side effects. Too much time at the hospital." He shook his head. "They have custody of a sixteen-year-old, Adam. Troubled kid who got arrested for drunk and disorderly twice last spring. He constantly pushes the boundaries. He's a good kid, though. Just struggling. Plus they have two other foster children. Not to mention they own and manage a bar. It's just a lot."

"It must be hard to balance all that. I'm not sure I could do it."

The words came out of my mouth before I thought better of them. I nervously wove my fingers through a lock of hair that fell over my chest, and when Jackson's eyes tracked the movement, I brushed it over my shoulder.

He cleared his throat. "Yeah, I admire the hell outta them. I thought maybe I could make a difference. I spent hours researching the fostering and adoption process here. Even watched a fucking orientation video."

I bit the inside of my cheek to stop from smiling. Now that I knew him a little better, I could picture that. Once he set his sights on a goal, he would give it 110 percent. Just like he had with the catering company.

"So what happened?"

His jaw clenched and unclenched twice before he spoke again. "Nothing. That's the problem. I hired an attorney to help me with the process, submitted my application, and nothing. My lawyer says I need to show more stability on paper."

"What does that even mean?"

"I need to show I'm a reliable adult. And prove I have ties to the area. Not just an investment, but a business, a steady job, even a wife. It's all risk assessment, and apparently, I don't look like a good bet."

I silenced the laugh that escaped me when his eyes narrowed. "Sorry, I don't see you getting married anytime soon."

"Yeah, no interest in a nine-to-five *or* compromising what I want just because it looks good on paper. But it's not enough for them that I'm an investor. I invest, then move on. What they don't see is that I work with business owners and help them buy their businesses back when possible. Like with Bill and Dani. They were some of my first clients, and their bar is successful again because I invested capital when they needed it."

Jackson's initial millions came from investing in an app similar to Candy Crush that had taken off over the last eight years. But that was the extent of my knowledge when it came to his career. Now it made sense. Jackson was a fixer.

"What are you doing to *fix* that?" Part of me knew that deep down, if this was what he wanted, he would figure it out. We shared that drive, the need to succeed.

He huffed out a breath and shrugged. "Hell if I know." He reached up, his hand swiping along the side of his neck. "I've been trying to get a community outreach program off the ground. Based out of Asheville and partnering directly with the children's hospital. But I haven't had the time to devote to it lately."

"What kind of outreach program?"

The waiter appeared with our starter before Jackson had a chance to answer, and before we were alone again, he shoved a piece of meat and a chunk of cheese into his mouth. I narrowed my eyes—was he purposely avoiding my question?

"Why don't you want to tell me?" I finally asked.

"It's not that—I don't know if it's shit or not. Brittney loves it and Rhett thinks it's great. They're biased, but you're not. You might say it sucks ass."

I blinked and then let out a laugh. "I'm not sure I'd be *that* harsh."

He raised one eyebrow, and the corner of his mouth tipped up. "Yes, you would." He slumped back in his chair and sighed.

My lack of filter and the need to tell things like they were could sometimes make for a bad combination. It hit me in that moment that I wanted Jackson to trust me enough to tell me.

"Come on, I'm not a soul crusher. Stop pussy footing around and tell me."

The tension ebbed from his shoulders as he chuckled.

"It's kind of a mix between Make a Wish and the Big Brothers Big Sisters. Simply put, the program would match a volunteer with a sick child. They'd spend time together, get to know one another. Other volunteers could offer services, like Rhett wants to give free boat rides."

A chuckle escaped my mouth. That sounded just like my brother, but I couldn't fault him. Between running The Dock and the instant family he and Bella had created in the last five months, he was all kinds of busy.

Jackson's jaw tightened and his lips pinched together.

Shit, he didn't think I was laughing at his idea, did he?

"I can totally see Rhett doing that. He's so busy he wouldn't have time to devote to physically volunteering out here. But I would love to. I enjoyed singing and I like to color."

I didn't have much else to offer, but I liked the idea.

His face relaxed and he blew out a breath. "Does that mean you don't think it's shit?"

"No, not at all. I think the families would appreciate that."

The waiter delivered our main courses, and Jackson talked more about his plans. Specifically, how he hoped it would prove that he was invested in our community enough to stay and enough to be approved for adoption. But we both knew he would need more, even though neither of us voiced it.

"Okay, princess, your turn." Jackson leaned his forearms on the table and regarded me closely, causing my core to clench. His intensity was back, and suddenly I was nervous again.

"My turn? For what?" My voice squeaked. I sounded

ridiculous, but seriously, what could I say about myself? That my goal was to set the perfect scene for other people's happy events? That sounded pathetic and shallow.

My aspirations would never come close to being as impactful as Jackson's passion for helping and doing more.

He had so much more of his shit figured out than I did, which was ironic. Two months ago, I thought he was an immature, self-centered playboy. Crow sandwich party of one?

His eyes narrowed before he shook his head. "I don't need a detailed life plan. I'm just curious about what sent you into a tizzy earlier. After the bakery. You obviously came to the same conclusion I did after you thought about it."

I heaved out a breath, not sure if I wanted to go there with him but relieved that I could avoid the insecurities that arose when I compared my achievements to his. Maybe he deserved *some* explanation. "I want to expand the catering business."

He chuckled, a low, sexy sound. "No shit. But that doesn't explain why you think I wouldn't understand that." He cleared his throat. "You're good at what you do, and I've looked over the finances. It's clear the decisions you make are leading the business in that direction."

I glanced down, tucking my hair behind my ear. "Hearing that it paid off was the highlight of my"—I blew out of a breath—"my month. And you're right. I wouldn't have upped the order on a whim, but you knocking it—"

His eyes widened and he shook his head.

"No, I don't mean it like that." I stabbed at the food on my plate with my fork. "I had a boyfriend who was controlling. He wanted my life to revolve around his dreams, and he was unsupportive and manipulating. I guess it's still a touchy subject for me."

"You were excited, and I was worried you'd jump the gun, but I should have known better. You've proven to be a good businesswoman. And I get where you're coming from. We all have shit like that in our past. I try not to let mine control me, but I'd be lying if I said it doesn't take over sometimes. Once someone you care about breaks your trust, it's hard to let go of that need to protect and defend yourself."

I raised an eyebrow. I wasn't sure I wanted to have this conversation with him, but my curiosity got the best of me. "I only remember you dating one girl seriously. The one you were with in the months before your car accident... the one who never showed up at the hospital."

"She would be the one; it took me six months to figure out she only wanted my money. Not me."

"Not even the 'mind-blowing orgasms' you rave about?" I said, thinking back to what he'd said at Rhett and Bella's wedding.

His irises went impossibly darker. Damn if I didn't want to find out exactly how mind-blowing those orgasms could be.

"I think a new pair of Louboutins were more her jam." He shrugged and looked away before schooling his features once again. But then a switch was flipped, and his gaze turned heated. "I guess the things my tongue could do were just an added bonus."

I crossed my arms, narrowing my gaze. "You know, you do that a lot."

"Do what?" His brows knitted together in the sexiest way.

"Deflect."

"Seems we have that in common."

"I'm cheap, but I have a shoe addiction," I blurted out. Maybe if I opened up, he would too.

"Okay..."

I chuckled. "I don't own *actual* Louboutins. I refuse to pay more than a hundred dollars for *any* pair of shoes. But if I total up my shoe collection, I probably *have* spent thousands of dollars. It's a real problem."

"I'm a judgmental ass. 'Cause I've definitely spent too

much on shoes and watches, not to mention my overpriced smart appliances. And you were right; although I got the Aston Martin for a steal, it wasn't cheap."

Our conversation continued naturally after that, our guards slipping a bit as we laughed and teased. After refusing to let me pay for my meal, Jackson guided me along the busy street toward his car.

His hand landed on the small of my back, applying pressure as he ushered me out of the way of a Vespa courier. A shiver ran through my body at his touch, and I stole a glance up at him. The corners of his mouth twitched, his fingers now digging into my hip, and his gaze locked on my lips as I traced them with my tongue.

Just as quickly as the moment happened, he released me. His jaw locked, and he broke our heated stare. I knew all the reasons we were both fighting this, but the more time I spent with him, the harder it was to ignore the attraction.

And I was ready to say screw it and embrace whatever this was.

Chapter Ten

JACKSON

"I THINK WE SHOULD DO IT," Ashley said as she stared out the passenger-side window.

"Do what?" If she was going to insist on upping the budget for that bakery after the conversation we'd had, we were really coming to blows. I grabbed my water bottle from the console and took a drink. It had been a long fucking day. But I had to admit, I'd enjoyed seeing Ashley relax and be herself.

"Screw."

I choked on the sip of water. The plastic bottle crinkled, and I jerked the steering wheel, causing the car to swerve.

"*Excuse me*?" I said once I'd gotten the car back into the correct lane. I couldn't have heard her correctly.

"We should get it out of our systems." She shrugged like it was no big deal. "It'll help relieve the tension."

Yeah, no.

Or... maybe.

I shook my head.

Think with the right head, man.

It was more likely that I'd get my ass kicked by her brother and she would end up hurt. Could she handle a casual hookup? Was that what I wanted? Another meaningless fuck?

"I could list a dozen reasons why that's a bad idea. Starting with Rhett. He'd cut my nuts off. And I'm quite fond of them."

"Pretty sure we can have sex without the whole town finding out. And it's not like we'll have to deal with each other once your mom is back at work." She rolled her eyes. "Stop being so dramatic."

I laughed at the absurdity of her statement.

"Right. It's not like my best friend, who is also your brother, is married to your best friend or anything." I scoffed.

She shrugged.

"You act like we'll never have to be in the same room together."

"And?"

Seriously? She was making me sound like the ridiculous one?

"Our moms are best friends, for crying out loud." I was spitting out any reason I could come up with, mostly because my dick was currently jumping up and down, begging for exactly what she was offering.

"I get your point. But we're adults. I think we can manage to have sex without making *everything* weird."

My dick did the happy dance at her logic.

Jesus.

"I don't do relationships."

There. That should work. She hated being reminded of my playboy status.

"Good, I'm not asking for one. I can barely tolerate you right now."

I threw my head back and laughed. "But you want me to fuck you?"

"Well, yes. We don't need to talk during it, you know."

"What if it's dirty talk?"

"Then it's fair game." She smirked.

I had to adjust myself when her pupils dilated, practically eclipsing her irises. Damn, the things I would say to her while she writhed under my touch.

"Look, Rhett won't find out. The last thing I want to do is come between the two of you. Bro code or whatever. It's just one time, and we don't have to make it weird." She nibbled on one long red nail before she caught herself and removed it. "I mean, unless you've changed your mind."

Fuck.

How do I respond to that? No, Ashley, I have not changed my mind. I've only been fantasizing about you for months. Hell, longer than that, if I was honest. But she was my best friend's sister and off limits. I needed to shut this down.

But for some fucked-up reason, I couldn't make myself say the words.

"You know I haven't." I ran my hand over my face and warred with myself. If I turned her down again, there was no way this firecracker would give me a third chance. But that was what I wanted, right? For her to remain firmly in the off-limits category? "But the last thing I need is for you to go and fall in love with me. Your brother will kill me if I hurt you."

She struggled to get her laughter under control as I glared at her. That was a first. A girl who only wanted me for my body. Not my money or the life I could give her or even my charming personality.

She covered her mouth with her hand, her laughter subsiding.

"Trust me when I say you don't need to worry about that," she finally said, then let another giggle escape.

I shook my head. And *I* was the dramatic one?

The next fifteen minutes were utter hell. The tension between us grew, and by the time I parked in the lot behind the catering building, I was holding on to my last thread of control. Every time she shifted in her seat, each time she crossed and uncrossed her legs, I ached to run my hand up her thigh and find out if she was wet. And every time she stuck her nail in her mouth, I imagined it was my cock.

She was a siren, a temptation I couldn't ignore. Calling me, captivating me.

The leather cracked when she shifted again, and my throat went dry as she slowly dragged her skirt up her thigh. I tightened my grip on the steering wheel in an effort to control the urge to reach out and follow the path her fingers were on, even licking my lips when she revealed lacy red panties.

Fucking little temptress, and the sexiest thing I'd ever seen. I threw my door open and stalked around the car. Once she stepped out, I had her pinned against the car. I leaned down so my lips were inches from her ear.

"You sure this is what you want, princess?" I slowly traced the shell of her ear with my tongue, and when she tried to close her legs, I used my knee to wedge them open again. "I like it rough. Is that what you want?"

Maybe somewhere in my subconscious I wanted her to say no. Hoped being pushy would scare her away.

But her breath came out as a moan. "Yes, Jackson. That's exactly what I want."

Her lips brushed against my neck, right where my pulse beat out of control. I fisted her hair and pulled her head back before my mouth crashed against hers. Itching to touch her, to feel exactly how bad she wanted me, I trailed a hand up her thigh, taking her dress with it.

But I pulled away abruptly, my inner voice screaming that we were in public in our small town.

"Inside, now," I hissed through clenched teeth.

She dragged her tongue across her bottom lip in a daze, and I grabbed her hand and pulled her toward the entrance to the catering office. I preferred a bed, but I wasn't waiting. The couch in her office—or the *fucking wall*—would do.

Ashley headed straight for her office and tossed her stuff onto her desk. I stood in the doorway, my hands braced on the frame, and followed her movements as she turned and slowly pulled her dress up and over her body.

I clenched my jaw and pressed outward, bracing myself as she regarded me from the middle of the room, wearing nothing but her knee-high boots, a lacy red bra, and a matching thong.

Before I knew it, I was moving, slamming the door and closing the distance between us. I pushed her against the desk, bracing one hand on it while the other explored her body. She let out a silent sigh as I traced one finger down her chest and unsnapped the clasp that sat between her tits.

I ran my fingers over her tattoo, eliciting a moan from her, her skin smooth under my touch.

"You're wound so tight, princess." My lips were inches from hers, our breaths mingling. "I want to watch you fall apart."

I flicked her taut nipple with my thumb, and her eyes drifted closed as a moan escaped her mouth. I crashed my lips to hers, pushing my tongue inside. When her teeth sank into my lower lip, I groaned and thrust my hips against her core, then broke the kiss. I needed to make her come. I wasn't sure how long I'd last once I was inside her. If this was the only night I got with her, I'd make it count.

"Look at me," I growled, slipping a hand under the waistband of her thong and sliding my fingers between her folds.

She's so fucking wet.

"Jackson, I—" Ashley panted, struggling to keep her eyes open.

"I know what you need, and I'll give it to you." I dipped one finger inside her, and then added another while I circled her clit with my thumb. "Nope. Eyes on me, princess," I said when she threw her head back.

The fire that burned within her when she looked at me was the sexiest thing I'd ever seen. I increased my speed and continued to rub against her tight nub at the same pace.

The moment Ashley let go of everything and completely succumbed to the pleasure I gave her was etched on my brain forever.

"That's it, Ash. Come for me." I curled my fingers and increased the pressure on her clit as she clenched around me.

She dug her nails into my shoulders as she came. The bite of pain made my cock pulse against her.

"Fuck, that was..." she breathed after the last waves of her orgasm subsided.

I smirked as I finished her sentence for her. "Mind-blowing?"

The need that still swam behind those hooded lids was like a punch to the gut. This girl was going to be the death of me.

"Very. Think you can do that again, but with your cock this time?"

If possible, the challenge in her voice turned me on even more. I stepped back, and with one hand, I pulled my shirt over my head and threw it to the floor while she removed her bra completely, along with her panties.

"Damn right I can." I gritted my teeth when she placed her hands on my chest and let them roam up to my shoulders and down my biceps.

She dragged her nails down my stomach, never breaking eye contact, and undid my belt and the button of my pants. I groaned when she grabbed a hold of me, her small hand gripping my cock.

I couldn't wait another moment. I made quick work of discarding the rest of my clothes. Grabbing her by the hips, I pulled her tight against my body. Damn, she felt fucking amazing pressed against me. "I can't wait to feel that tight pussy pulsing around my cock."

With a hand on my chest, Ashley pushed me back until my calves hit the edge of the small couch, forcing me to sit.

"Condom?" she asked as I tugged her closer, both hands on her hips.

"In my wallet." Shit, I was rusty. I'd almost forgotten. I never forget. What the fuck was she doing to my head?

I closed my eyes, hissing as Ashley rolled the condom on, and dug my fingers into her hips while she straddled me and sank down until I was fully seated inside her.

"Ride me, hard." I growled through gritted teeth.

She pushed up on her knees and then slammed back down on my cock, holding nothing back. I grazed her nipple with my teeth when I took it into my mouth, and she rewarded me with a moan that drove me forward.

"Fuck, Jackson. That feels—oh my god…"

I loved her lack of complete sentences as my thumb found her clit, firmly pressing against the hard bud. She increased the tempo, her tits bouncing to the rhythm she'd set.

"Ash—need you to come." I clenched my muscles, attempting to hold back. But when my balls tightened, I moved my thumb faster against her and tweaked one of her nipples. "Princess, you feel too fucking good."

The prick of her nails digging into my chest and the way she threw her head back as her pussy clenched around me had me taking over so I could finish with her. Furiously, I bucked my hips and groaned as her spasms triggered my release.

Ashley collapsed on top of me, face buried in the crook of my neck. I instinctively ran my hand through her hair and down her back, the act feeling way too intimate. As if she had the same thought, she sat up straight, and I internally groaned when she pushed up, removing my cock from her soft heat.

"I'll be right back," I said, making my way to the bathroom in the hall to dispose of the condom. Splashing water on my face, I looked in the mirror. Fuck, what had I done? And what the hell was I supposed to do now?

Would she really be good with going back to the way we were before? That sat like lead in my stomach. The idea of seeing her every day and not touching her again. Was that what I wanted?

When I stepped back into Ashley's office, she was gone, and so were her clothes. She hadn't run out, her stuff was still on the desk, so I quickly got dressed to go in search of her. Her phone vibrated on the desk as I was shrugging my shirt on, and without thought, I glanced over.

Rhett.

Talk about a reminder of what was at stake.

"Here." Ashley tossed me a bottle of water when she walked back in.

"Thanks. Rhett's calling." I nodded in the direction of her phone.

She groaned but picked it up.

"Hey," she said before her eyes went wide. "*What*?" She spun away from me. "What do you mean hurt?"

Fuck. Was it Brendan?

"How the hell don't you know?"

Not Brendan then. He would obviously know.

Maybe their dad? I hated that I couldn't interject.

"Okay, how's Mom?" Ashley turned back to me and rolled

her eyes before raising her voice another octave. "What the fuck, Rhett? Never mind, I'll go check on her." She disconnected the call and gathered up her stuff, then pushed past me.

"Hey, what's going on?" I said as I followed her out the door. Her family was like my own, and there was no way I'd let her leave without telling me.

"It's Kyle."

Shit. He'd been deployed for the last five months. That could mean anything.

"Ash, wait." I grabbed her wrist, turning her to face me. She was doing her best to school her features, but she couldn't hide the fear in her eyes. "Is he..." I swallowed over the lump in my throat, "he okay?"

"Alive, but no one knows anything. I gotta go. I need to check on Mom." She pulled away from me, and without another word or glance in my direction, she climbed into her car and drove off. And for the second time in twenty-four hours, I was left standing in this exact spot, watching her drive away.

I pulled out my phone. I couldn't call Rhett. What would I say? *I was fucking your sister when you called. How's Kyle?* Bella would just cry, and I still wouldn't have had any additional information. Savannah was off the table—with her big mouth, the whole town would know I called her within minutes.

My phone vibrated in my hand. Thank fuck, it was Rhett.

"Hey, man," I said once I slid my thumb over the Accept button.

"Hey." Rhett sounded tired, but instead of asking about what was going on, I waited for him to continue. "You busy?"

"Nope, what's up?" It wasn't a lie. I *had been* busy with his sister, but I wasn't anymore. How the hell would I ever look him in the eye again? I grabbed the back of my neck and was only half listening as he filled me in on what was going on.

My thoughts were a jumbled mess. Of all the ways I imagined things would happen after Ashley and I finally screwed, this was not one of them. And yes, I had imagined it. More times than I'd like to admit.

It was what we'd wanted, what we'd agreed to. Just tonight. Nothing more.

So why did I feel so unsettled?

Chapter Eleven

ASHLEY

My phone vibrated on my kitchen counter as I stirred pumpkin spice creamer into my coffee. Glancing over at Bella's name on the screen, I cringed. I loved her like a sister but, *shit*. I had just spent the last thirty-six hours dealing with all of them. Sitting with Mom and Dad and helping with whatever I could. Mostly just being there in case there was bad news. Not to mention fielding my siblings' phone calls and listening to the millions of questions we still didn't have the answers to.

I needed a break. But I couldn't say that. Everyone depended on me to handle it. I debated letting it go straight to voice mail, but what if it was something important?

I'm fine. It's fine. I've got this.

After leaving Jackson standing in the parking lot on Sunday night, I went straight to my parents' house. My mom was a mess, cleaning every surface while she waited for another update.

My dad was useless—without Mom telling him what to do, he had no clue. Normally, Kyle and I handled emergency situations together, but he had to go get himself injured and leave me to deal with these people. Rhett was no better than my dad when it came to needing constant direction.

It made sense. When we were kids, Kyle had been in charge of keeping an eye on Rhett and me while Mom dealt with Hattie and then shortly thereafter Savannah. Then, once Kyle and Rhett were school age, I became the "big helper."

But now, when Kyle wasn't around, the responsibility fell solely on me. I loved my siblings, and we each had our strengths, but to them, I was known as the mom whisperer. Maybe because I could sense what she needed, whereas the others had to ask.

I shook my head and grabbed for my phone. It probably wasn't Kyle related anyway. We spent most of yesterday together, and we all heaved a collective sigh of relief when Kyle called from the military hospital in Germany. He was going to be okay despite the gunshot wound to his leg that shattered his femur and the frightening amount of blood he'd lost due to the injury. The surgery was a success, but he might need another one down the road.

"Hey," I said after swiping the screen to answer her call.

"Hi." Silence followed, which wasn't normal for Bella.

"What's wrong?"

"Can you watch Brendan for me today? I'm in a bind."

Wait, what? I really tried not to sigh, but I was tired. Although I loved my nephew, I didn't know that I could handle chasing a toddler today.

"I thought you were working from home for the next couple of weeks." I worked to keep the annoyance from my tone.

"I am. But I have one client who is adamant about keeping our appointment today so I can show her around The Dock. Mom said she would watch B, but he's sick, and with everything Mom is dealing with, I don't want to drop a sick toddler on her."

As long as Kyle stayed in stable condition, he could be back in the States by this time next week, and my parents planned to drive to Bethesda this weekend so they could be there when he arrived and bring him home. They were prepping the guest house for him, which I'd also been roped into helping with. But they were both mentally and physically exhausted, so they didn't need a sick toddler today.

"Okay—"

Before I could say anything else, Bella went on.

"I'm about to just tell this client I can't do it, and with the fever B is running, I don't even want to leave him. What if..." I could hear the emotion bubbling up fast in Bella's voice. Brendan had been rushed to the hospital only a few months ago when he'd had a febrile seizure, so Bella was nervous anytime he had a fever.

I had no interest in doing what Bella did full time. My passion was the cooking, not the event planning, and The Dock provided all the food for the events. Dealing with clients wasn't always a walk in the park, but at that moment, it was more in my wheelhouse than dealing with a sick toddler.

"How about you let me meet with the client? That way, you can stay home with B."

"Really? Don't you have to go into work today?"

"At some point, but this week is a light one. I can meet with your client and then go into the office to put my supply order in. It's probably a better idea than leaving me in charge of a sick child. Don't get me wrong, I love B, but we both know he'd rather snuggle with you than me."

"Yeah, probably..." She was quiet again. I hoped she wasn't crying. Between her and Mom, I was drained.

My *there, there* voice would come off as *I don't give a shit* if I tried to affect it at this point. And I really did give a shit. I was just... exhausted.

"Why don't you email the details? Whatever I need to know. I'll handle it, okay?"

A sniffle came through the line, and I closed my eyes. *Fuck*.

"Thank you, Ash. I really appreciate this."

"No problem. Spend the day snuggling with B and watching TV. You both probably need that."

After hanging up with her, I opened my text message thread with Jackson. My thumbs hovered over the keys like they had three other times since Sunday night.

What would I say?

I convinced him things wouldn't be awkward, but here I was, at a loss for words, which was rarely an issue for me.

Jackson had been just as radio silent, which wasn't in character for him either. Rhett had probably already filled him in on the Kyle situation, but I found myself hoping—ridiculously—for a *how you holding up?* text.

Brushing off my thoughts, I sat at my computer and pulled up the email from Bella so I could go over the details of the family reunion this client was looking to host at The Dock.

Later that afternoon, as I climbed back in my car and headed toward the catering office, I was even more drained. Bella's client was a pain in the ass, to put it mildly. But I put on my best fake smile and sold her on how my family's restaurant and inn was the best location in Half Moon Lake to host her family gathering. But if she had complained one more time about the size of the patio area, I probably would have lost my shit and told her to find a different event space to accommodate her needs. But I'd promised Bella I would take care of it, so I did.

It reinforced, though, that I wanted to cater big events like that one, but part of me doubted that Callahan's Classic Events would ever get there. Hotels or places like The Dock that offered lodging accommodations as well usually hosted the larger events.

I parked on the street in front of the row of stores and businesses where our office was located. Victoria Myers, one of our regular clients, approached just as I reached the entrance.

"Hey, Ashley, I was hoping you'd be here. I emailed you, but when I didn't hear back, I figured I'd just swing in," she said before quickly adding, "I know your family is dealing with a lot. We're so sorry to hear about Kyle. You let us know if there's anything we can do, okay?"

Shit. I hadn't checked my emails in days. I was so far behind, and it would take me days to catch up.

I nodded. "Of course. Come on in. How can I help you?"

Opening the door to the small lobby of the catering building, I let Victoria walk in front of me. The bell above us chimed, and I motioned toward a table where we met with clients to go over menus and pricing. Before I followed her, Jackson came out from the hall where our offices were located and stood behind the counter. Our eyes met, and my stomach flipped.

"Hey," he said with a tight nod.

"Hi." It was unnerving to be at a loss for words around him. Not to mention how my body buzzed under his inspection in ways I wasn't prepared for. Looked like we needed to talk after all. "I'm going to meet with Mrs. Myers for a few minutes," I finally said.

"Okay, I'll be in my office if you need me." He gave us both another nod before turning and retreating.

I sat across from Victoria and went over the details of the

Christmas cocktail party we were catering for her in early December. The menu she had in mind was more involved than what she usually requested. I zoned out a few times, but I got the gist. Her husband was up for a promotion, and she wanted to impress his boss.

An hour later, I stood in the open doorway of the office that Jackson was temporarily using. When he didn't look up, I cleared my throat.

"You need something?" He glanced at me and then focused on the invoices in front of him before checking his phone. His whole demeanor was off. Like an out-of-sorts, stressed version of laid-back Jackson. His attention bounced from the screen to his phone again before locking on me once more.

God dammit. I should have checked in before now. That was the text I should've sent the three times I considered it.

I suck.

"Do you need help with something?"

"Not really. There's a discrepancy with one of the vendor invoices. I'm waiting for them to call back."

His phone rang, and he snatched it up. Looked like neither of us had time to dissect what had gone down between us. I needed to lock myself in my office for a few hours and play catch-up anyway.

Chapter Twelve

JACKSON

I WATCHED Ashley's ass sway as she walked out of my office, all but tuning out the voice on the other end of the line.

I tried to focus on the invoice issue, but my mind kept drifting back to Ashley. I had wanted to check on her so many times since Sunday night. But fuck if I knew what to say.

And yeah, this whole crazy idea of sleeping together had been a bad idea. I knew it, but I'd gone along with it anyway. Sex *always* complicated everything. We needed to put it behind us and continue to work together the best we could until my mom was able to step back in.

After dealing with the invoice issue, I turned off the computer and gathered my stuff. Ashley and I needed to talk, but I didn't have it in me to face that elephant at the moment. Between covering things here for the last two days and the invoice problem tonight, there was no way I was in the right frame of mind.

Because the part of me that wanted to bend her over her desk would not shut the fuck up. I didn't trust myself not to cave to that desire, so I made my feet move through the kitchen and out the back door.

Once I locked the door behind me, I shot off a text to my buddy Dylan to see if he was free to grab a drink.

Twenty minutes later, I sat at the bar nursing a beer while I waited for Dylan. He was the sergeant of our small town's police department, and I'd caught him at the end of his shift.

A loud collection of feminine laughs came from the back corner of the space. Glancing over, I took in the scene. Looked like a bachelorette thing. One woman was wearing something ridiculous on her head, a mix between a crown and a veil. Women were so weird. I didn't recognize any of them, so they were likely tourists.

At one point in my life, I would have been over there by now, trying to determine which of them were single. I'd hooked up with my fair share of tourists. They usually weren't looking for anything other than a one- or two-night fling, and I didn't have to deal with running into them over and over again in our small busybody-infested town.

A punch to my arm jolted me out of my thoughts, and I spun to face Dylan, who'd planted himself on the stool next to me.

"Which one you have your eye on for tonight?" Dylan said with a smirk and a nod to the girls.

I shrugged. "They seem like they've been at it for a while, so even if I was interested, I wouldn't be taking any of them home tonight."

Dylan surveyed the loud, drunk women and came to the same conclusion. He gave me a nod, and then his eyebrows shot up again. "What do you mean *if* you were interested? The tall blonde seems like your type." He picked up the beer the bartender placed on the bar and brought it to his mouth. His eyes went wide, and he sent me another smirk. "Oh shit. Incoming." he said, indicating what I assumed was one of the girls from the table behind me.

I felt rather than saw a figure sidle up to the bar and brush against me. I kept my back to her, hoping she was just ordering more drinks.

"Excuse me," she said.

I turned slightly and raised my eyebrows at her. She was gorgeous. I had to admit that. Long, blond hair and green eyes. But the image of another blonde, one with blue eyes that went stormy when she was angry or turned on, was like a punch to the gut.

Fuck.

"Are you local? We were wondering if there was a place around here that has live music," the blonde asked, not so subtlety giving me a once-over.

"Sorry, not tonight. The Crescent Moon will have a band tomorrow night, though."

She smiled and brushed her hair over her shoulder. "That's great, thanks." Her speech wasn't slurred, and her eyes weren't glassy. She must have been the sober one who'd been tasked with driving the obnoxious group of women. I almost felt sorry for her.

"No problem." I turned to Dylan again, who had a *what the fuck* expression on his face, while she ordered another round of drinks.

"Your dick broken or something?" Dylan said after she'd gone back to her friends and he'd picked his jaw up off the floor.

"Nah, man. I don't know. I'm just not in the mood." That sounded even more lame than it did in my head. But there was no fucking way I could tell him that I fucked our friend's sister and now I couldn't get her out of my head.

His eyes narrowed on me like he wasn't buying it, but he didn't push, just took another swig of his beer and turned back to the bar.

I breathed a sigh of relief. "So how's—shit man, I'm sorry, what's her name?"

Dylan rolled his eyes. "Nice to see some things haven't changed. And *Becca* is fine. I don't see it working out, though."

I laughed, 'cause that was such a Dylan thing to say. "Remember what I told Rhett when he dated Sarah for three fucking months and kept saying that same thing?"

"Yeah, yeah, but this is different. I wouldn't mind if it worked out. I just don't think she can handle the cop thing long term. She complains about the hours and when I can't take off for things." He shrugged and effectively ended the conversation when he flagged down the bartender and ordered a basket of wings.

With another sip of my beer, I did my best to distract myself from my reality by focusing on the game playing on the screen above the bar.

Maybe tonight I could fall into bed without the images of Ashley riding my cock haunting me.

Chapter Thirteen

ASHLEY

THE WIND WHIPPED the hair away from my face as I walked to my car. I should have been relaxed now that I was finally caught up on work, but no. Instead of a night off, I had to cover a party. After taking a few days for Kyle and my family, I would have done this party tonight without complaint if Jackson had just asked. But *Asshole Jackson* was apparently back and even more of a dick than before. What the *fuck* was his issue?

Don't get me wrong. I didn't expect some elaborate conversation about what happened between us. But *damn*. I wasn't imagining things; we did sleep together, right?

And I wasn't prepared for him to go straight back to being a jerk.

I swallowed over the lump in my throat. If that was the

way he wanted to play it, that was *fine* by me.

Once in my car, I pulled up the texts from him, gritting my teeth as I read them *again*.

> Jackson: You have to take over tonight's event.

> Me: What, why?

> Jackson: I can't be there.

> Me: Why not???

> Jackson: I fucking can't, okay? Just do it.

I was too angry to respond, but there was no way I'd let a client down. I'd considered asking Kelly. She'd been requesting more hours for the upcoming holiday season, but springing it on her last minute wasn't cool. On top of that, this wasn't her only job. She was an Uber driver, and Fridays were probably her busiest nights. She was a few years younger than me, and she was a bit of a hot mess, like my sister Savannah. Responsible with great work ethic, but not super organized. And with Christmas coming up, she was scrambling to make extra money.

I spent most of the afternoon prepping, loading the van, and dropping it all off at the high school for the PTA event.

As I breathed a sigh of relief that I had pulled it all off, my fingers flew across the screen.

> Me: Where are you?

> Jackson: Home.

Three dots appeared and disappeared multiple times

before they stopped completely. A one-word response? Really? I waited another minute, but *screw it*, we needed to talk. And in person, where I could scream and maybe throw things at him. He owed me an explanation. He may have been used to getting away with shit because he was so good-looking it physically hurt, but he was in for a rude awakening if he thought he could pull this shit without a good reason.

I slammed my fist against the door after knocking three times with no response. Finally, he answered, wearing only a towel, his hair still wet and water dripping down his bare chest.

Shit, is he with someone?

Maybe this wasn't the smartest idea I'd ever had. The last thing I wanted was to be confronted with what I'd known when I'd gone into this. It wouldn't be long before he hooked up with someone else. It was what he did. And I'd known it when I made the decision to sleep with him, so I had no right to be upset. But less than a week later?

That stung.

I swallowed thickly. I wanted so badly to remove the image of each of his tattoos from my memory. But my traitorous eyes inspected his chest, which was adorned with the rendering of a lake surrounded by trees. Half Moon Lake. The mountains in the background covered his left pec and shoulder and continued over his bicep. He had music notes along his rib cage. Both of his forearms were covered, and there were a handful on his back and legs. I didn't know why they drew me in, but I wanted to know what each meant.

Glancing over his shoulder and then back to his face, I opened my mouth to tell him what an asshole he was, but he cut me off before I spoke.

"I'm sorry. I know I was an ass earlier." He stepped to the side and waved me in.

I stood frozen in place with my hands on my hips. He

turned and moved farther into his house, leaving the door open and me unsure about what to do.

After a brief hesitation, I followed him to his kitchen.

He jumped into an explanation, spitting the words out quickly. "I was a jerk. I know it. I apologize. But I forgot about the event when something—"

I stopped him with a hand up. "Go get dressed, please."

His usual smirk almost appeared as he knitted his eyebrows in surprise. "Why? You've seen it all now, princess, remember? I think we can take modesty off the table at this point, don't you?"

"If you want me to hear your apology and your lame excuse, then I need you to put some fucking clothes on." I folded my arms across my chest and glared at him. I could not have a serious conversation with this man when he was almost naked.

"Fine." He turned and left the kitchen, then returned wearing a pair of basketball shorts and a T-shirt a few moments later.

How he looked even more sexy with clothes on I couldn't understand, but I wasn't about to tell him that.

"Okay, you were saying you were an asshole...?" I prompted.

He blew out a breath. "Sophia's back in the hospital. She got worse again. Her blood tests were off yesterday, and they're worried the cancer is back. I wanted to see her after she went in for her bone marrow biopsy this afternoon." He grabbed the back of his neck and squeezed while his head fell forward. When he brought his eyes back up to meet mine, his shoulders fell and the mask he usually held in place finally came down. The reminder of the fierce love he had for this little girl lodged hard in my chest. "I forgot about the event until I was about to walk into the hospital. But it doesn't excuse the way I acted. I was just frustrated and worried. I'm sorry."

"Oh." If he'd told me that, I would have understood, but I couldn't be upset with him knowing Sophia was sick. "When will they get the results from the biopsy?"

"Monday or Tuesday. Possibly sooner. Her oncologist isn't too concerned, but they want to rule it out. Give us peace of mind, I guess."

"I'm sure, and I hope her doctor is right, but keep me updated, okay?" I asked as my stomach made a loud, fairly unladylike growl.

Jackson's eyes narrowed. "Have you eaten today?"

I shook my head. "No, I didn't have a chance. Some jerk demanded I drop everything and do his bidding." I softened my jab with a flirtatious tilt of my head and pursed lips.

"If I wanted you to do my bidding, you'd be on your knees."

My tongue traced along my bottom lip, and heat flooded my body. I wasn't opposed to that idea now that he'd mentioned it.

"Fuck, Ash. Sorry, I shouldn't have said that." He adjusted himself and turned away from me. "I'll whip us up something. I haven't eaten either."

"What is that supposed to mean?" I narrowed my eyes at his back. The hot and cold was grating on my nerves. Pick a lane, for Christ's sake.

He spun back toward me, his eyes hardened, bracing for a fight. "What part? My apology or making us something to eat? You can go if you don't want to be here."

I was getting whiplash. "Why are you being weird? We fucked, and now you're making sexual innuendos but then acting like you're crossing a line. Talk about hard to read." I blew out a breath and rolled my eyes.

He stared at me like he was waiting for me to say more, but I didn't elaborate, and I didn't break eye contact, calling his bluff.

"You done?" he finally asked.

"No, I'm not, actually. You didn't even call or text and ask about Kyle."

"Last I checked, you had a phone too, princess. You could have updated me. Luckily, *your brother* had the decency to fill me in, and I took care of everything at the office, even though you didn't ask." He crossed his arms.

Maybe he was right there. It was unprofessional of me not to follow up with work stuff. Barbara and I would have checked in with each other.

I sighed. "I didn't know what to say. 'Thanks for the mind-blowing orgasm. My brother is fine. How's work?' didn't seem right."

He smiled then, and I narrowed my eyes. What did I say to cause that cocky smirk?

"Orgasms. Plural." He smirked. "They *were* mind-blowing, huh?"

Oh my god. I wanted to strangle him. "Yes, and you know that. But then at the office, our interaction was awkward and you brushed me off."

His brow furrowed. Men are stupid was the conclusion I was coming to at that moment. He looked like Rhett anytime one of us was upset with him. I laughed and shook my head.

"Not sure what the protocol is when you fuck your best friend's sister, okay? I wasn't sure if I should text or call or neither. At the office, I think I was just focused on what I was doing, and I wasn't sure how to go back to being just friends."

"So we're friends now?"

"I figured after you rode my cock, we were more than just two people who hated each other."

I nodded. "I guess that's true."

"We both know it can't happen again, though. Hence the reason I apologized for the sexual comment."

"I know." I nodded again. "Didn't you promise me food?

As a thank you for covering you tonight?"

He nodded. "Hey, Alexa," he called into the air, cocking his head to the side. "Play some country music."

Morgan Wallen's "You Proof" played from his smart refrigerator. Of course he'd have kitchen appliances with built-in speakers. Why wouldn't he?

"Do you always listen to music?"

"Most of the time. It calms me down. So if it's been a shit day, yeah, I'm putting it on." He moved around the island and pulled out different vegetables and fresh chicken from the fridge. "I usually relate to the lyrics in some way or another, and I hate the quiet. So I always have something playing."

I walked around to his knife block and pulled out a chef's knife.

"What are you thinking? I can help."

"How about a chicken pasta primavera?"

"Okay. Want me to chop the broccoli and peppers?"

"Yeah, and I'll pan fry the chicken."

We worked well as a team in the kitchen. The more time we spent cooking together, the more that became clear. I fought back a smile when "Learn From It" came on and Jackson sang along. And before I realized it, I found myself joining in too.

His love for music was infectious.

Once we had everything finished, I plated the food and carried our dinner to the table. Jackson opened a bottle of wine and joined me.

"Your skill in the kitchen is impressive, Ash," he said, filling our glasses, then hesitating before adding, "What happened with culinary school though? Are you planning to go?"

My fork clanged against the plate when I dropped it. I stared at it for a moment before I met his intense stare and that stupid, sexy grin of his.

"I'm happy with what I'm doing. I don't see the point."

"I don't believe that for a second. I think you're scared, but I'm not sure if it's because you failed once already or because some ass said you're not good enough."

My mouth dropped open. Who the hell did he think he was?

"You know this is one of the reasons I've never liked you, right?"

"Why? Because I'm honest to a fault? And I don't beat around the bush or sugarcoat shit? Pretty hypocritical coming from you."

I shook my head and bit the inside of my cheek to stop from laughing. "Touché."

"Did you just admit I'm right?" His eyes popped wide as he threw his hand comically over his heart.

"Even a broken clock is right twice a day." I rolled my eyes at his antics. I twisted a piece of hair around my finger and took a breath while I contemplated the best way to answer. "I don't think I'm scared. Maybe when I first came home after college, I was. But I'm happy working for your mom now. And I don't think I could work full time like I do and go to culinary school and be successful at both."

"Makes sense. But if you wanted to try again, my mom would be willing to work around your schedule. You know that."

I nodded. "Maybe."

It felt weird to be encouraged so openly like this. My ex constantly put me down, telling me culinary school would be a waste of time and money. I still regretted letting him influence my decisions, but at the time, I was blind to his manipulative tendencies. I'd been a fool to let my love for someone blind me to signs I should have seen.

"What did you study in college?"

"Business. I thought I wanted to follow in Rhett's footsteps. Come home and run the family business alongside him. But I quickly realized I wanted to cook. So your mom's offer was literally the best of both worlds."

"Why didn't you go to culinary school after you graduated?"

I didn't want to go there. We weren't involved. At best, we were coworkers, even if he'd referred to us as friends. But I didn't need, nor want, to spew my baggage at him. And it wasn't easy for me to talk about—being reminded of how often I felt less than and the words my ex used to confirm that he never thought I was good enough. That no matter what I did, it was never *enough*.

"That's a conversation for a different time."

He raised his brows. "But—"

I was quick to shut down where this was going. "I don't feel like revisiting past shitty relationships tonight. Just let it go, Jackson."

"Alright, I hear you loud and clear, princess."

"And stop calling me that," I snapped. "If you want to be friends, you could start by not annoying me every chance you get."

"I think it's sexy when you get all riled up, though," he said with a wink.

I rolled my eyes and went back to my dinner. But I couldn't help the grin that broke out across my face. Maybe Bella was right when she told me he did it on purpose. Was it his version of flirting? Did that actually work on other girls? It would be different if we were teenagers, but we had long since grown up.

On my drive home, I replayed the night in my head. Shit, I replayed the last few weeks. I was playing a dangerous game doing that, and it scared me. There was too much at stake. I needed to think with my head and not let my attraction to him cloud my judgment.

Chapter Fourteen

JACKSON

Sitting next to my mom in a church pew on Sunday, I couldn't help but let my attention drift up and over to the blond head of curls. After years of spending summers on the lake with her family, I knew Ashley had naturally straight hair. Recently, and more times than I'd like to admit, I'd thought of her hair after a day on the boat and how it gave her that just fucked look. Images of what her face looked like a week ago when she came flashed across my mind.

I'm going to hell.

I was thinking of sex with my best friend's sister while in church with my parents. That was a new low, even for me. I bowed my head along with everyone else, praying specifically for the strength to stay away from Ashley.

Once the service was over, I weaved through the throngs of

people, making my way to the one person I'd just resolved to avoid, the woman who had a magnetic pull on me.

"Ash," I said when I was close enough to get her attention.

She spun, and her smile grew. And damn, that was a sucker punch. She rarely greeted me with a smile. Usually, I got resting bitch face. At best.

"Where's your mom?" She glanced over her shoulder and then back to me. "Your parents were with you, weren't they?"

"Yeah, but her back was starting to bother her, so they left."

She nodded and then looked around at the people milling about. "Did you—I mean, were you going to ask me something?"

I bit back a laugh, because she was almost unsure. Like she was trying extra hard to think of what she was saying. Which was so unlike her.

"Yeah—are you planning to do any prepping today?"

"No. I was going to test out those salmon and goat cheese phyllo bites. Why?"

"I had an idea for a new sauce. Thought maybe you could be my taste tester?"

She narrowed her eyes—clearly unsure about why I was angling to spend more unnecessary time with her—and I sure as hell didn't know either. "I could try the phyllo bites for you. Win-win."

My cock took notice when she brought one long finger to her mouth and nibbled on her nail. I shifted my weight on my feet, suddenly rethinking my suggestion.

"Okay—" Her hand came down and landed on her hip. "Your place or mine?"

"Mine." I spat out before I could think any better of it. Knowing the real reason I wanted her at my house, in my kitchen. Or the shower. My hot tub. My bed. *Fuck*. And all the reasons this was a bad idea came flooding back once again. "Mine is nicer and bigger than yours." I shot her a cocky grin.

"Ugh, you're annoying." Her bottom lip jutted out, and I resisted the urge to lean over and pull it into my mouth with my teeth. "But also, once again, right."

"I'm always right."

She rolled her eyes. "Let's not get carried away."

I laughed.

Hattie came up alongside her sister, glancing between the two of us. "Look at you guys being all friendly. What are we talking about?"

I raised my eyebrows, and the corner of my mouth twitched. "Just seeing if the princess here can help me later."

"I asked you to stop calling me that," Ashley said through gritted teeth.

Yeah, fat chance in hell. I loved watching her eyes blaze when she was annoyed. Especially now that I knew her eyes lit the same way when she rode my cock.

"Okay. Before we're asked to leave because you two start bickering like a married couple, I'm hungry. Can we go to lunch now?" Hattie directed at Ashley.

"Yup, let's go." Ashley turned away from me, tossing her hair over her shoulder. "Text me what time you want me there."

Driving away from the church fifteen minutes later, I second-guessed what we were doing. I knew what I wanted. And part of me knew what would happen tonight if she came over. I was pretty sure she knew it too. But neither of us wanted to stop it, did we?

I stopped in to have lunch with my parents and almost choked on my food when my mom said she had been thinking about liquidating the catering business like I'd suggested before her surgery.

I gulped my water, trying like hell to clear my airway.

Fuck my life.

"Excuse me?" I said when I felt confident enough to form words.

"You were right. It was a passion, and something I've enjoyed doing. But let's be honest. Even when I'm back on my feet, it'll be hard to enjoy it the way I used to."

"I get that, but I—I guess I assumed you would have Ashley take over when you were ready to retire."

"No offense to Ashley, son," my dad interjected, "but no. I never argued about the expense because it made your mom happy. But we're barely in the black, and paying another employee to cover for your mom will make that a losing venture."

"I... weren't those my exact words over the summer? And then again in September?"

"Yes, honey. I know." My mom placed her hand on my forearm. "And I appreciate you putting your traveling on hold to help me out—"

"Barbara," my dad mumbled, stopping her.

My jaw clenched. Because, of course, they thought I only traveled for pleasure. At least she didn't mention my lack of having a real job. That was usually her go-to.

She sighed. "I didn't mean it like that. Dad made it clear that the trip you canceled to help me was for business." She squeezed my hand. "I appreciate that you stayed here to help me out."

At least we were moving in the right direction. My father mostly understood and was more interested and supportive in my investing. It wasn't exactly what he had done with the stock market, but he saw the similarities. Even if he wasn't convinced my original investment in an app was a wise decision and not dumb luck. They'd both been strongly opposed when I invested part of my trust fund into my buddy's idea.

But I saw the trend, and he had an impressive idea and the skill to bring it to fruition.

I didn't blame my mom. She just didn't get it. Every time I tried to explain how investing in the software program had been lucrative, she made some implication that I got lucky, or that she didn't understand how a person could profit from a free app.

"It's fine," I finally mumbled. "I know how much your business has meant to you. So I'm a little surprised you want to liquidate now."

"I know. This injury has reminded me that I'm getting old. I probably should have listened to you when you brought it up before."

"You know Ashley's going to be pissed, right?"

"She'll be fine." She waved me off like I was exaggerating. I hoped that was the case. "I haven't made up my mind yet, but I'll talk to her. I'll let her finish out the events we have scheduled for next year, so she'll have plenty of time to find something else. And of course we'll give her a glowing recommendation."

I shook my head. It wouldn't be enough. Ashley would be devastated. She saw it as so much more than a job; I understood that now. But it wasn't up to me, wasn't my decision. And Mom was probably right. Ashley would be fine in the end. Maybe this would be the push she needed to go to culinary school.

We spent the rest of lunch talking about Thanksgiving. Brittney was adamant about hosting, and I understood her reasons, even though it was an inconvenience to me. But, fuck, Brittney was right. If we had it here at Mom and Dad's, Mom would feel obligated to cook and do more than she should, but Ashley and I had a few orders to prep and deliver that day *before* I could even leave to make the hour-drive to my sister's. I could crash at Brittney's so I didn't have to drive the hour back that night, though. Maybe I could stop and visit Sophia while I was in Asheville.

Standing in my kitchen later that evening, I stirred the creamy lemon garlic sauce I had brought to a simmer. I'd texted Ashley earlier to be here around six and to just let herself in.

My whole body tensed as the snap of the front door closing and her soft footfalls echoed her presence. Glancing over my shoulder, I tracked her movement as she entered the kitchen with a bright smile that had me transfixed.

"You okay?" Ashley brushed a hand down my arm, sending an electric current coursing through my veins and my dick jumping in my pants.

Slowly, I drank her in. She wore tight black leggings and a wide-neck tee that slipped off one shoulder and didn't cover her stomach, leaving a few inches of skin exposed.

What the hell was she trying to do to me? The conservative dress she wore to church earlier with the leggings underneath would have been so much easier to ignore. At least it covered her ass and stomach. The curls were gone now, too, and instead, she had her hair twisted and secured in a tight bun on top of her head.

"What the hell are you wearing?" were the only words I seemed capable of forming at the moment.

Her eyes widened before her lips formed a tight line and the glare I had become so familiar with bored into me. "Clothes. I didn't realize there was a dress code."

"Those—" I waved at whatever the fuck she was wearing. "I would *not* call clothes. Clothes cover your body and keep you warm when it's cold outside." It wasn't freezing, and she probably didn't need a jacket. But it wasn't seventy-degree weather either.

She continued to glare at me until one eyebrow rose and the corners of her mouth curled up slightly.

"Unless I'm mistaken, I'm pretty sure *you're* the one who said we can take... wait, what did you call it?" She brought one blue fingernail—a perfect match to those cerulean eyes—to her chin in a dramatic *I'm thinking* fashion. "Modesty? That was what you said. We can take *modesty* off the table now."

I growled as she moved to the end of the island with a little more sway in her hips than usual. Ashley had a tight little body. She was tall and thin, not too many curves, but *fuck*, that ass. It was probably the only part of her that could be considered curvy. And in those damn tight leggings, I wanted to bend her over and...

I'm so screwed.

Shaking my head, I focused back on reducing the sauce.

I snuck glances over at Ashley while she unpacked ingredients, preheated the oven, and cut the phyllo dough into squares before finally placing them in the tart tins. Music floated around us that played softly from the refrigerator, and I wasn't sure how much more of this I could take. The way she moved her hips to the music, as if it were as natural as breathing, had my dick growing impossibly thicker. I bit the inside of my cheek when she bent over and put the dough in the oven.

"You're gonna burn your sauce if you keep staring at my ass," Ashley teased.

"Shit," I mumbled. She was right, and the sauce was sticking to the pan.

Damn it to hell. This woman would be my undoing.

I turned off the burner and moved it to the back of the cooktop.

"Don't have such a fine ass if you don't want me to get distracted. Or maybe if you wore actual clothes..." I said after turning back to face her.

She rolled her eyes like I was ridiculous. Did she know how irresistible I found her?

"Right. Clothes. I'll try to remember that next time." Her

tone was thick with sarcasm as she mixed the ingredients for the goat cheese filling.

It was time to move on to neutral territory and get my head—*both* heads—off images of sinking into her.

"Your parents made it to Bethesda?"

Rhett had called yesterday to give me an update on Kyle. His parents planned to drive to Maryland today so they'd be there when Kyle arrived from Germany. He would likely be discharged later this week, and his parents would then drive him home.

"Yes—I talked to my mom on the way here. They just got there."

I grabbed a clean knife and sidled up next to her to slice the salmon into thin strips.

"Rhett said he has some extensive rehab ahead of him."

"He'll be fine. He's like me. Determined and stubborn."

I threw my head back and laughed. Yeah, that sounded about right.

At the sound of the oven timer, I turned and removed the tins of crispy dough. "What's next?" I asked, placing the baking sheet on a cooling rack and hitting the Off button to silence the timer.

"Those need to cool before I fill them." She placed her bowl of filling and the salmon strips in the refrigerator.

"Can I try the sauce?" She nodded toward the pan cooling on the cooktop.

"Not sure if it's any good, but yeah..."

We walked the length of the rectangular island to where the electric range sat across from the sink. Stacked double ovens were built into the wall separate from the stovetop, which allowed use of both without running into each other every five seconds.

I scooped a spoonful of sauce and held my hand under it to catch any drips before bringing it close to Ashley. Our eyes locked as I brought the spoon to her lips. I'd never thought that watching someone take a bite off a spoon could be sexy, but damn, in that moment, I wanted nothing more than to put my mouth where the spoon had just been.

She licked her lips, and after I set the spoon on the counter; I brought my hand up to cradle her jaw and wiped a drop of sauce from the corner of her mouth with my thumb.

That magnetic pull was back, and I found myself leaning in.

"Needs more lemon. And a pinch of tarragon." Ashley's breathy voice flowed between us.

"Huh?"

"The sauce."

"Right, tarragon. Good catch." I didn't give a fuck about the sauce at that point. The only thing I cared about was getting my mouth on her. My cock ached where it bulged against the zipper of my jeans. I should've removed my hand and stepped back. But I was too far gone, captivated as her eyes darkened and her breathing went ragged. And, fuck, did that make me want her even more. "I shouldn't kiss you."

I knew I couldn't, but I was leaning in anyway, our lips only inches apart.

"Probably shouldn't," she said in a whisper.

"We agreed. We can't do this again." I froze, searching her expression, giving her one more chance to stop this.

"I know, but I don't care."

Fuck it. I grasped the nape of her neck and pulled her to me, crashing my mouth against hers. Applying just enough pressure, I tilted her head and deepened the kiss. Her warm lips welcomed me as I hungrily devoured her.

Ashley was a hellcat. There was no doubt about that. But when she was in my arms, it was a beautiful surrender.

Chapter Fifteen

ASHLEY

THIS WAS SUCH A BAD IDEA, and we both knew it. But Jackson's hand on the back of my neck and the way his mouth dominated mine made me want everything he was offering. Even if it was only here and now. Over the last week, I had touched myself so many times, thinking of the way Jackson played my body like the guitars he was so familiar with.

When I sucked on his bottom lip, he responded with a husky groan that vibrated through me and shot straight to my core. Palms flat, I slid my hands under his T-shirt and around to his back. His cock twitched against my hip as I dug my fingernails into his skin. Just like the last two times we'd kissed, this wasn't gentle or tender. It was desperate and greedy, like neither of us could get enough.

His lips left mine, and a whiny sound I never imagined I'd make escaped me.

He chuckled against my throat as he sucked and nibbled on the sensitive flesh. "You needy, princess?" he mumbled, grazing my ribcage with his fingertips.

"Yes." I whimpered and wished I wasn't wearing this damn sports bra when he roughly grabbed my breasts.

His thumb brushed against the front zipper of my bra, then skated over my nipple. I swear I almost came from that touch alone.

"Fuck, you're so responsive," he said before his lips were bruising mine again.

He moved quickly, unzipping my bra so he could circle my hard peaks with both thumbs. The tension built so fast I thought I would explode. I stepped closer, removing every inch of space between us, seeking friction. As if he could read my mind, he wedged his thick thigh between my legs.

I rubbed against him, and the pressure built quickly in my core.

I dug my fingernails into his back when he tried to pull away, and he surrendered, continuing his assault on my mouth and nipples while swiftly moving us around the island. Before I could protest again, he broke the kiss and spun me, his hands gripped tightly on my hips. My breath caught, and I pressed my ass back against his hard erection.

"You're not coming against my leg, princess. You'll come when I'm buried inside you." He moved one hand to cup my breast while the other slid low and rubbed me where I ached for him most. "Bend over and put your hands on the counter."

I'd do whatever he wanted if it meant he would drive into me.

With both hands planted firmly on the cool granite, I glanced over my shoulder. Jackson was disappearing through the archway that led to the front of the house. Where the hell was he going?

Before I could rethink what we were doing, he reappeared and threw a condom on the counter next to me. I tracked his movements as he undid his jeans and pulled his thick cock out. Slowly, he ran his hand from base to tip, his eyes never leaving me.

"Jackson, please. I want you inside me."

"I like this needy side of you," he growled as he continued to stroke himself.

I'm not sure I do.

But he was right. I *needed* this more than I needed my next breath. I might have hated how desperate I was for his touch, but it didn't make it any less true. His hand landed between my shoulder blades, applying just enough pressure that I braced my forearms on the counter.

A shiver shot through me when, in one fluid motion, he yanked my leggings and thong down my legs.

"*Fuck,*" I moaned, all but melting into a puddle on the floor when he glided himself along my seam, rubbing against my clit. I was already so close. The moment he entered me would likely send me over the edge.

He grabbed the condom, and then a second later, I felt him line himself up to my entrance. His fingers were digging into my hips, and I screamed out when he drove into me in one solid thrust.

I slammed back against him each time he moved forward, seating himself deep inside.

"Damn, this ass. Do you know how many times I've imagined doing this?" He kneaded each globe as he pulled them apart each time he pushed inside.

"Probably as many times as I have since last week." I threw my head back as I met his thrusts.

He stilled and dipped down until his chest pressed against

every inch of my back and grazed my ear with his lips. "No, princess. You don't understand. I've fantasized about this since way before last week."

I gasped at his words, but before I could analyze them, his fingers were circling my clit.

His name on my lips was a breathy moan as my orgasm hit me with a force that left me shaking. Two more powerful thrusts, and he was following me with his own release. I collapsed on the counter. The coolness of the granite through the thin material of my shirt reminded me that we were still mostly dressed.

I'd never had an experience like this—a mutual need so urgent that obstacles like clothing had been completely ignored. A fluttering sensation swept through me and landed in my stomach when Jackson's fingers brushed a few stray hairs off my cheek.

"You okay? That was fucking intense."

I smiled. Jackson always said whatever came to his mind. It was actually refreshing. And he was right—that was probably the best sex I'd ever had.

"I'm not sure I can stand. My legs feel like Jell-O."

He laughed, and his dick twitched inside me. He kept his hands on my hips, supporting me as he pulled all the way out and then worked my thong and leggings back up my legs.

"I'll be right back."

Once I was confident my legs wouldn't give out, I turned and plopped onto a nearby stool and zipped my bra back up.

I need to go to the gym more often. Or do more yoga or something.

Jackson strolled back into the kitchen with a cocky-ass grin on his face.

I raised my brows at him and shook my head. "Yeah, yeah. That was amazing," I said as I clasped his outstretched hand

and let him pull me to my feet, praying my legs would hold me up.

He leaned forward and traced my ear with his tongue. Another tremor of pleasure flowed over me.

"I want to do that again and again," he whispered.

I swallowed the lump that rose in my throat. I wanted that too, but how would it work? He didn't do anything more than casual. And me? I had no interest in getting involved with someone, especially my brother's best friend. So maybe we could pull off just hooking up.

He straightened to his full height so that I had to tilt my head back to look up at him. That intense stare of his burned into me.

"Jackson, I—"

"Don't worry. It's fine. I get it. You're right, we shouldn't do this again." He turned and walked around the island before I could respond and grabbed a pot from the rack. He filled it and placed it on the burner, all while avoiding eye contact.

"That's not what I was going to say."

He turned and leaned against the counter, arms crossed over his chest and legs crossed at the ankles. "No?"

"No." I moved to stand in front of him. "The sex is amazing. And if we set some ground rules, I don't see why we can't continue enjoying it."

His brows hit his hairline and his eyes widened. When he didn't respond, I continued.

"Let's say, what, six weeks? We go our separate ways after the first of the year. Then you can find your next *flavor*."

He narrowed his eyes and clenched his jaw at my suggestion. Was six weeks too long? I guess most of his "flavors" were only around for a few weeks.

"Or shorter than that if you want. I figured we have to work together until then, so—oh—and no sleeping with other people while we're hooking up. That's a deal breaker for me. When you get bored, just be up front about it."

"Why do you assume I'll get bored? And you know your brother will kill me when he finds out."

I ignored his first statement. His track record over the last ten years spoke for itself.

"No one can know. Not my family, not your family, not our friends. *No one.*"

"I'm not sure that'll work."

I shrugged. "Those are my conditions. Take them or leave them. I don't see why we should tell people we're having casual sex. It's fine for men, but I'll be judged, and you know it."

He actually looked guilty. He knew I was right.

I put my hands on my hips and waited for a rebuttal. The way he clenched his jaw and stared at me told me he had more to say.

"Fine," he said with a sigh. "On one condition, though."

"Hmm?"

"If at any point we decide to tell people or someone finds out, let me talk to Rhett. He needs to hear it from me."

I bit the inside of my cheek. Why he would want to have that conversation with my brother was beyond me, but they were best friends and honored bro code and all that, I guess.

"Fine. But no one is going to find out, so there will be no need."

His hands landed on my hips, and he pulled me tight against him. Something hard pressed against my stomach, sending another wave of heat through me instantly.

"I'm agreeing to this only because my dick is making the decision right now. But I'm going on the record to say that this is a *very* bad idea."

Typical guy.

I rolled my eyes. "It'll be fine. We both know this'll keep

happening. This way, we're in agreement on how we handle it, right?"

He nodded. "Whatever you say, princess."

I huffed a breath through my nose. "Now I *know* you're thinking with your dick."

He chuckled, and I pulled away from him and headed to the fridge so I could pull out the goat cheese and salmon.

"I'm going to whip up some pasta to go with this sauce. Sound good? Our new rules don't say anything about us sharing a meal together, do they?" Was he purposely trying to irritate me?

"You still need to try my salmon and goat cheese phyllo bites. So yes, might as well have pasta too."

I tried to ignore the way he examined me as I filled a pastry bag with the mixture and piped it into the cups. Then I shaped each piece of salmon to the best of my ability and placed them on top of each phyllo cup filled with the goat cheese.

"That's smart—using the pastry bag to fill the cups evenly."

"Thanks."

We ate the phyllo bites while we waited for the pasta to cook. Jackson was great at giving constructive feedback on taste and texture and suggestions for next time. The chives would be a good idea. I wasn't sold on adding nuts.

After we ate and cleaned up, I sat on one of the stools, sipping my second glass of wine.

"Is there a limit in your rules for how many times we can fuck, like, at a time? Or is this an unlimited plan?" Jackson asked with that cocky smirk plastered on his face as he loomed over me.

He braced his hands on the island on either side of me, effectively caging me in. If he wasn't so goddamn sexy, and if my stupid hormones didn't like the sound of round number two, I would have called him an asshole and stormed out. But he was, and I did.

Maybe I could torture him a bit.

I shrugged. "I don't know. Do you think you'll be able to *perform* again? I mean, you're what, almost thirty-one? Maybe your stamina isn't what it used to be." I tried to hide my smile behind my wineglass as I took a sip.

"I'll show you stamina," Jackson muttered, taking the drink from me and setting it on the island.

"Hey, I wasn't done with that."

"And I'm not done with you."

I let out a squeal when he put both hands under my ass and lifted me up. I scrambled to wrap my legs around him as he carried me out of the kitchen and down a long hallway.

I bounced on the mattress after he tossed me in the middle of the enormous king-size bed in his master suite.

"This time I want you fully naked and under me."

The thought of being completely bare and spread out on his bed half excited me and half scared the shit out of me. As he stripped down to nothing, his gaze intent on me, the thought crossed my mind that I might be in over my head.

But I wasn't going to walk away. Not today. Eventually, this had to end. But for now, I'd enjoy every single orgasm he was willing to give.

Chapter Sixteen

ASHLEY

MY FEET and back were so fucking sore. Yeah, I really should have looked into a gym membership. Between the extensive sex sessions with Jackson and standing in heels so much over the last week, my muscles were stupidly tight. I plugged my phone into the car when the low battery sound chimed again, and a new text message lit up the screen.

> Jackson: Come over after your event. I
> need my fill.

I smirked and bit the inside of my cheek before responding.

Me: Only if we can soak in your hot tub.
You promised me two nights ago, but we
got sidetracked.

Jackson: I didn't hear you complaining.

Me: Well, my thighs are definitely
complaining now.

Jackson: …

Me: Do not say it. I am NOT working out
with you.

Jackson: …

Me: I'm going home.

Jackson: No, you're not.

Jackson: Get your ass here. I'll have the hot
tub and a glass of wine ready.

Me: Need to run home to change and grab
a suit.

Jackson: Why? We're going to get naked
anyway.

I rolled my eyes before my fingers flew across the screen again.

Me: I want comfy clothes. Be there in 20.

My apartment was on the way to his house, so it would only take a few extra minutes to grab a pair of sweats and my skimpy bikini. Teasing Jackson a bit with it might be fun.

Thirty minutes later, I was in heaven. Not only did Jackson make good on his promise, but now I was sitting between his legs as he rubbed my shoulders. I could practically hear my muscles sighing with relief.

"Hear me out before you say no, okay?" Jackson leaned forward, his lips close to my ear.

The rough timbre of his voice awakened the need for him that always floated just below the surface. I leaned into his touch a little more.

"No promises," I mumbled as I closed my eyes.

"Brat," he said before nipping my ear with his teeth, eliciting a moan from me. "Let me show you some stretches. Not a workout; just stretching."

I popped my eyes open, ready to tell him to go to hell. But I lost all train of thought when he trailed his warm lips down my neck while his hand journeyed down my side and across my stomach, pressing me into him farther.

"Jackson," I murmured.

"Is that a yes?"

Wait, what was the question? Oh. Stretching. Yeah. Hard no.

"Still a no."

Jackson didn't respond, which was out of character for him, but then he grabbed my thighs and pulled them apart. I gritted my teeth to hide the wince but let out a sigh when he kneaded the sore muscles with his thumbs.

"I guess I'll have to go easy on you if you can't keep up."

Did he think his empty threat was going to change my mind?

"That isn't going to work."

"Princess, that's where you're wrong. You really liked that one position, and I was hoping to do that again. But there's no way you're holding a squat."

Fuck. He was right. And it didn't look like I would anytime soon. My thighs were still fucking killing me. But damn, that position was oh so nice.

"I hate you."

"Nah, you just hate to admit when I'm right."

I laughed before tipping my head back until it met his chest.

"Probably." I blew out a breath. "Fine. You can show me a *few* easy things."

He chuckled into my hair. "How did the fundraiser go tonight?"

"It was okay. Kelly was a godsend." A few minutes later, after filling him in, my conversation with Kelly came to mind. "You've been to Rockefeller Center, right? Like to see the Christmas tree?"

"Yeah. Mom tried to take us every year when we lived there. Where'd that come from?"

"Kelly and a few of her girlfriends are doing a bus trip up there next month." I closed my eyes, sagging a little so my shoulders were submerged. "I want to go one year. It's been on my bucket list."

The quiet almost lulled me to sleep until Jackson spoke softly again.

"We could go."

"Hmm?" I was too relaxed to comprehend the words.

"Fly up there after Christmas. Get a hotel for the night. Make a weekend of it."

I sat up so fast the water splashed violently around us. Turning to face him, I searched his face for a clue that he was messing with me. But his furrowed brows and tilt of his head said he was a hundred percent serious.

"That's insane."

We couldn't. And even if I was willing to consider it, how the hell would we both leave town without raising suspicion?

"Why?" The line between his brows deepened.

"I envy your ability to just *go* and *do* whatever you want whenever you want, but—"

"I think I just care a hell of a lot *less* about what people think." He shrugged. "But seriously, think about it. I'll make it happen."

"Why? Why would you do that?"

"Why not? I like to travel. I would love to see the tree in New York again. Show you around a little, go to my favorite pizza place. And then spend all night worshipping your body in a fancy hotel room. Nothing about the idea sounds bad to me."

"Besides lying to our families and sneaking out of town, hoping that no one puts two and two together."

"Again, *I don't really give a fuck about what people think.* Well, I care about our families, I guess, but that's it."

I shook my head. A day in the life of Jackson Vargas. It would be nice to care less some days.

I studied him for a minute. "You remind me of Savannah in that regard."

"Nah, I do what I want without caring what people think. But your sister purposely does stuff to garner reactions from people."

"Probably." I chuckled.

I circled back to the start of our conversation about New York and rapid-fired every question that came to mind. Now my curiosity was piqued. Why was it so easy to talk to him? He showed me the half sleeve tattoo on his right forearm, explaining why each thing was significant to New York.

"Tell me about the big tree. Is it as big as it looks on TV?"

"Are we talking about the Christmas Tree in Rockefeller Center again?"

I nodded. "Yup."

"No one calls it the *big tree.*"

I shrugged, and he chuckled at my expense, then went on about New York, visiting the *big tree*—now he was just making fun—and ice skating with his mom and sister at Rockefeller Center.

"Where do you put your tree?" I studied the exterior of his large two-story home. The whole back of the house had floor-to-ceiling windows that overlooked his patio. Besides his kitchen, this was where Jackson's style was the most prominent. With the pool, hot tub, covered bar area, outdoor kitchen, and firepit with plenty of seating, it was entertainment central.

He shrugged. "I don't usually put one up."

I sucked in a breath. What kind of person doesn't put up a Christmas tree? My brain spun with ideas about how I could convince him to do it this year.

"We need to get you a tree."

My gaze drifted to the far right of the house, where the great room with a cathedral ceiling was located. In front of the windows of that one wall would be the perfect place for a tree.

Jackson rolled his eyes, but I climbed onto his lap, wincing at the burn in my thighs.

"I don't know about a tree, but this is why it's important to stretch."

I huffed. "Shut up and kiss me, *asshole*."

"Whatever you say, *princess*."

Chapter Seventeen

JACKSON

The whole *AGREEMENT* thing we'd made was ridiculous, but that didn't mean I hadn't taken every opportunity to sink inside her. Between the office, my house, and her apartment, I'd had more sex in the two weeks since we'd made the arrangement than I had in the whole year before. And not only that, but with Ashley, it was off the charts. We were so hot for each other that it was always needy and desperate.

Like tonight. The minute I stepped into her apartment, I pinned her against the wall and took her right there because I couldn't wait a minute longer. She was like a fucking drug I couldn't get enough of.

But the ridiculous part was that it wasn't just the sex. I liked being around her, making her laugh, talking with her. It was... refreshing. I'd never met a woman who engaged my mind while also revving up my body. But Ashley was turning out to be exactly what I'd spent the last year and a half searching for. And here I was pretending I was just her secret hookup or friend with benefits. Whatever label she wanted to give it.

But when she directed that smile at me, I didn't care what she called it, as long as I could be here. Especially because what we were doing felt a lot like dating to me. Apart from the actual *going out on dates* part.

Because no one could know. And I couldn't fuck her on the table in the middle of the restaurant. Thus there was no way to convince her that going out made sense for our situation. So I bit my tongue and continued to play this her way.

Why? I wish I knew.

Ashley had put the fish in the oven, and I was making Spanish rice to go with it. I shook my head as she sang along to "Down to One" while we made a late dinner. And even though it was a sappy fucking love song, I could relate to the need for just one more night with this girl.

"I need another hot tub session," she said as she spread her legs and bent over into a nice stretch. I smiled, loving that she was using one I'd taught her the other day.

I had to resist the urge to pull those tiny booty shorts down to her ankles and slam inside her *again*. I felt like a teenage boy as I adjusted my painfully hard cock.

But seriously, why couldn't she ever wear fucking clothes? Images of her in a skimpy bikini a few nights ago flashed through my mind. Relaxing in the hot tub with her as we sat and talked had been the perfect end to the day. When she'd climbed onto my lap, I was content to just kiss her. Until she ground herself against me and I'd been forced to carry her inside and give in to her demands.

She stayed over that night. She'd fallen asleep on my chest, and fuck, it made my head spin. I couldn't remember the last time I didn't want to immediately untangle myself from a woman after sex. But with Ashley? Fuck. I was in trouble.

She was pissy the next morning, though, because I hadn't woken her up. What did she expect me to do, wake her up in the middle of the night and send her home? Yeah, wasn't happening.

That wouldn't be casual. That would be me being a dick.

"Why don't you come over tomorrow night and we can relax in the hot tub again?" I suggested, stirring the rice and keeping my focus off her ass.

"I could do that every night. I'm so jealous that you have access to a hot tub at all times."

"I told you to come use it anytime."

"I know..."

We moved around her very efficient kitchen—everything had a place, and her system was even more organized than mine—as we put the finishing touches on dinner.

"Would you, um, want to watch a movie tonight? Like after we eat. Or if you need to go, that's fine too."

I couldn't help but chuckle. She was one of the most confident women I'd ever met. But occasionally a hint of vulnerability would peek through, and I found that version of her just as sexy.

"Sure, sounds good."

We were moving into uncharted territory, and she knew it too. Even if she wasn't ready to admit it. I'd agreed with her silly rules at first, but I had no interest in ending things after New Year's *just because*. This wasn't a casual thing anymore, and she'd realize that soon enough.

She'd created a timeline and expectations because she was protecting herself, and that was why I didn't push. And don't get me wrong, I wasn't ready for the white dress and babies, but what we had was perfect, and I didn't want it to end come January. So I had six weeks to make her see that she should give us more time. Let things happen—or not—naturally. No pain, no gain—wasn't that the saying?

"Have you seen Kyle?" I asked once we were almost done eating. I settled back in the chair and stretched my legs out under the dining room table.

"Not really. He's closing himself off from pretty much everyone. Doesn't want to come up to the main house, doesn't want us bugging him or hanging around. Mom says he'll come around, but..." Her brow creased as she tucked a piece of hair behind her ear and took a sip of her wine.

"But you don't think so?"

"Kyle and I are a lot alike. If it were me, and I lost something that gave so much value to my life, I'd be angry and distance myself too. I've been there, and it took a long time to pull myself out of it. I couldn't handle the pity, and part of me wonders if that's how Kyle feels."

Shit. The conversation with my mom came to mind. Is that how Ash would feel if she lost the catering business? She was passionate about expanding it, but maybe she would see it as a push to go to culinary school. I wanted to give her a heads-up, but it wasn't my place, and I hated the idea of it coming between us.

I replayed her words, letting my curiosity get the best of me. "What do you mean you've been there?"

"My ex... the manipulative one." She looked away, refusing to meet my eyes.

"Yeah. You mentioned him."

"It ended pretty badly. We lived together. I gave up a lot so I could stay in Atlanta with him. I was stupid. Thought he wanted to marry me. That he loved me. I realized after the fact that he'd fed me bullshit for years, only saying what he thought I wanted to hear rather than being honest with me."

Those words were a sucker punch to the gut. It wasn't the same, right? That wasn't what I was doing. I was giving her time to realize that maybe what we had was more than just sex. I would tell her that eventually, but for now, I was happy to let things play out like she wanted.

"My life literally revolved around him." She blew out a frustrated breath and gripped the table so hard her knuckles were white. "But no matter what I did, it never seemed to be *enough*." She picked up her fork again, moving the food around her plate.

I didn't want her to shut me out. I needed to understand why she was so skittish about relationships.

"What happened?" I probed.

She was quiet and continued to stare at her food. I was convinced she wouldn't give me any more insight into the situation with her ex, but then she finally spoke again.

"It was little things at first. He would convince me his choice of restaurant was better or come up with a completely plausible reason for why we never got together with his family. Or why he couldn't attend things that were important to me. Even when he convinced me that moving in with him instead of sharing an apartment with a friend made more sense. But when he was adamant about me holding off on culinary school until he was more established in his career, I got that first feeling that something wasn't right. But by then I was so used to jumping through hoops to please him that I went along with it yet again."

I clenched my jaw, determined to let her talk and fighting the urge to tell her how much of a selfish ass her ex was.

"It wasn't until five months later, when I broached the subject again, that I said enough was enough." She finally lifted her head, and anger blazed in her irises. "He had the *nerve* to tell me he didn't think I could be a *good wife* if I was busy chasing silly, stupid dreams, and that he should have listened to his mom when she told him I wasn't good enough for him."

"You were *too* good for him."

The anger slowly ebbed from her face and was replaced by a frown.

"I felt like such an *idiot* when I came home—like, who doesn't realize when they're being manipulated? I told my mom if one more person said *it was for the best*, I was going to punch them in the face." She huffed out a chuckle.

"I won't say that, but he definitely didn't deserve you." I brought the lip of my beer bottle to my mouth and took a swig before adding, "I get it, though. You're too hard on yourself. But you were young, and you're probably the *take no shit* person you are now because of that."

"Anyway," she deflected, "back on topic, which is Kyle. I think he'll need to find another purpose before he can pull himself out of this hole he's in. But I pray I'm wrong." She shrugged and picked up her fork again, effectively ending the conversation. Every time I got a glimpse behind those walls, she was quick to throw them back up. This was the most vulnerable and open she'd been with me, so hopefully I was slowly chipping away at the fortress she liked to hide in.

Two hours later, I had one arm on the back of Ashley's sofa and the other wrapped around her shoulders. She'd fallen asleep with her head on my chest an hour into the first *Lord of the Rings*. The movie fanatic that she was—something else we had in common—she'd suggested starting the trilogy tonight.

Her soft snores made me smile. I considered waking her up since my cock was begging to be inside her again, but she had gotten up at five to prep a large order, so I'd let her sleep a while longer, then carry her to bed. If she woke then, I could bury myself in her soft, wet heat one more time before going home to my empty house.

Ashley felt right in my arms, but I couldn't silence my

doubts about how it all would play out. Between keeping this from our friends and families and the questionable future of the catering business, I wondered if it would all implode.

We were playing with fire, that was for sure. But as long as Ashley came out of it untouched, I didn't care if I got burned.

Chapter Eighteen

ASHLEY

I STARED at the extra place setting as I put the salad bowl on the table. Sunday night dinners were a ritual in our family. If we were in town, we were expected at our parents' house each and every week.

But my stomach was spinning like one of those gravity-defying carnival rides because I wasn't sure I could pull this off.

Tonight, I had to sit across from Jackson and hope everyone believed that I'd missed church this morning because I hadn't felt well. Because I couldn't tell them the truth—that Jackson had me in the shower, making me scream his name as he drove me to the brink and back multiple times with his mouth before fucking me. In my defense, we'd gotten in the shower set on going to church. But after our escapades and

Jackson's offer to cook breakfast, I texted my mom and told her I couldn't make it.

"Jackson's coming to dinner tonight," my mom said as she placed a basket of rolls on the table.

She didn't know that I was with Jackson this morning when Rhett called and invited him. The look on Jackson's face when I came into his kitchen and said his name, not knowing he was on the phone with Rhett, was priceless. He played it off, insisting it was the TV and asking Rhett why the fuck he thought he'd have a chick there on a Sunday morning. Apparently, Rhett bought it as I stood there with a hand over my gaping mouth. Jackson found it hard not to laugh, but I did not find it funny in the least.

"Oh? He is?" I cringed at the unfamiliar higher pitch to my voice. This was going to be harder than I thought. I hadn't ever been super forthcoming with information where it pertained to my personal life—I preferred to keep most things private—but not once had I truly needed to lie or hide things from my family, especially my mom.

But if they found out, the damage would be irreversible. Our mothers would start planning our wedding, and we sure as hell weren't doing that or anything remotely close. Rhett would pull the big brother *I can't believe you're fucking my sister* shit with Jackson. Which, by the way, would be so hypocritical since he was married to my best friend.

But what-*ever*.

"Ashley, did you hear anything I just said?"

Whoops. I finally looked over at my mom and cocked my head because, nope, I had no clue what she was rambling on about.

"I'm sorry. I, um, still have a bit of a headache from this morning."

"Mm-hmm." My mother's eye roll said she wasn't buying my crap. If anyone was going to figure it out, it was her. No one knew me like her except Bella. But Bella had a lot going on, and she would let me have my privacy even if she suspected something. It was just the way we were. We knew when to push and when to back off. "I *was saying* Rhett and Jackson are visiting with Kyle for a while. Hopefully they can convince him to come up for dinner."

"That'll be good. Maybe they can get through to him."

Kyle was doing well on his crutches but struggling with the potential of a medical discharge from the Army hanging over his head. According to Mom and Dad, his prognosis was great, and he'd be reassessed after physical therapy, but Kyle was convinced this was the end for him. Of course my dad's response was "it is if you see it that way." He never sugarcoated shit, that was for sure.

She nodded. "Everything okay at work? You must be worried that maybe Barbara will close up shop and retire."

"What?" My eyes had to be bugging out of my head. The last thing I needed was one more derailed plan. I blew out a breath—never thought I'd miss my routine, boring life. "Why would you say *that*? Di-did *she* tell you that?"

"No, no." My mom waved her hand in the air. "Nothing like that. I just figured you'd be worried about it. The recovery has been harder than she thought. Do you think she'll come back full time once she's recovered?"

"I don't know. But I've talked to her about taking on more if she needs to step back."

Great. Keeping my relationship—or casual hooking up or whatever we were labeling it as—with Jackson a secret was the least of my concerns. It hadn't even crossed my mind that Barbara might not keep the business going. It wasn't a multi-million-dollar thing, but we made a profit each quarter. I felt the niggle of a migraine coming on just thinking of the possibility.

"What is it, then? I can tell something's on your mind. Is it Jackson?"

I whipped my head around. "What?" There was no way she knew. "Of course not. Why would you think that? I—"

Her eyes went wide. "I know you two don't get along, so I worried there might be a problem there. But now..." She pursed her lips as she examined me.

I bit the inside of my cheek. Shit. Could she see it written all over my face?

"Is my wife here yet?" Rhett asked, thankfully pulling Mom's attention away from me as he entered the dining room behind us and bent to place a quick kiss on her cheek.

"Not yet. Where's Jackson? I thought he was staying for dinner." Her gaze landed on me again, searching for the answer like I had it. "Did you scare him away?"

"Huh? Jackson said things were going well." Rhett's attention shifted back and forth between us.

"Did he, now?" One corner of my mom's mouth turned up.

"I didn't *do* anything—everything's fine." I huffed. "I'll bring out more of the food." I turned and all but sprinted into the kitchen as Rhett asked my mom what my problem was.

Smooth, real smooth.

Bella and Brendan came in through the front door when I stepped into the kitchen, and Rhett and my mom's voices joined them a second later.

Jackson's whisper came from the mud room as I moved around to the far side of the island.

"I'll be there by three or four."

A feeling I wasn't familiar with hit me, causing my stomach to flip. Who was he talking to? Where was he going? And more importantly, why did I care?

"And I can stay the night?"

I pinched my eyes closed. I had no claim on him. But fuck,

we'd agreed not to sleep with other people while we were doing this, and I'd made it abundantly clear that he only had to let me know when he got bored and wanted to move on. I should've known Mr. Playboy couldn't keep it in his pants. I was so fucking stupid. Feelings I hadn't experienced in over five years hit me like a ton of bricks.

"Okay, sounds good. Love you," he said after another moment.

Huh. I practically scoffed out loud. That couldn't have been another woman because Jackson didn't do love or relationships. Maybe it was his mom. But why would he need to stay there? I stepped inside the dimly lit room, and the minute I did, his gaze whipped to mine and a cocky grin, the one that always sent a jolt straight to my core, broke out on his face.

He grabbed me by the waist and pulled me tight against him, his mouth crashing down on mine. The risk of being caught should have worried me, but all the nerves I'd been dealing with faded away as his tongue explored my mouth.

I gasped when he gripped my ass and lifted me onto the counter that lined one wall. He tangled his hand in my hair, tilting my head before his lips trailed down my neck.

"Fuck, I can't get enough of you."

I smiled at his words and threw my head back when his hard cock rubbed against the juncture of my thighs. Damn him.

"You had me twice this morning."

He groaned in response, rotating his hips and making me squirm. I placed my hands on his shoulders, pushing him away.

"We need to stop before someone walks in," I said, but I missed his touch the moment he stepped away. I bit back a smirk as he adjusted himself. "Who were you on the phone with?"

"My sister, confirming Thanksgiving plans."

Relief hit me first, but then annoyance—not with him, but with myself. I shouldn't have been so bothered. This arrangement would be over by the new year, but he'd promised me he wouldn't sleep with someone else while we were hooking up, and I took that seriously. That was all.

He glanced toward the kitchen, voices catching his attention. "We should probably get in there."

"You go first." I nodded in that direction.

He looked down at his still obvious erection. "I might need a minute."

Smiling, I hopped down off the counter and left the mudroom.

"There you are," Mom said as she held out the dish of mashed potatoes. "Carry this in the dining room for me, please." She nodded toward the sliding barn door that separated her kitchen from the dining room.

I nodded. "Okay."

Taking the bowl from her, I pulled away but froze as her eyes went round. Of course Jackson walked out of the mudroom at that exact moment. Her grin grew wide, and I did my best to keep a straight face.

"Perfect timing, Jackson. Do you mind carrying the ham in for me?" She nodded to the platter layered with ham sitting on the island in front of me.

"Sure thing, Mrs. Williams," he sputtered as his neck turned red.

"Oh, stop that. How many times have I told you to call me Miranda?"

"Sorry, Mrs. Williams. It's just a habit after all of these years."

How the fuck had I never noticed how adorable he was when he was being polite? Whoa, why the hell was I finding him adorable all of a sudden? I'd heard of voodoo pussy. Was there such a thing as voodoo dick? That had to be my issue.

Jackson and his dick's ability to give me an infinite number of orgasms were messing with my head.

Dinner went smoothly at first. Jackson and I sat at opposite ends of the table. I swear he glared at me when I didn't take the seat across from him. But it was safer up at this end.

"Jackson, have you decided whether you're going to your sister's for Thanksgiving?" my mom inquired. "The last time I spoke with her, Barbara said you weren't sure."

"Yeah, I think so. Ash and I have orders to prep that morning."

My head snapped up at the mention of my nickname, one he had never called me before a few weeks ago. I didn't dare look at anyone else, but out of the corner of my eye I could see Bella studying me.

Jackson, of course, continued on like he hadn't slipped up. "So I don't love driving an hour after working all day, but yeah, that's my plan."

"You're welcome to join us for dinner if you'd prefer."

No. Fucking. Way. I wasn't doing this again.

"No," I blurted before I could engage my practically nonexistent filter.

All eyes turned to me, and I immediately regretted my gut reaction when Jackson's jaw clenched and he was now the only one *not* looking at me.

Fuck my life.

"I mean, I'm sure Brittney and his parents want him to be there with them. Didn't I just hear you talking to your sister? I thought you mentioned staying the night."

His eyes finally met mine, but the intensity radiating from him had an angry edge.

"Eavesdropping now?"

"I was in the kitchen. Not my fault you were loud enough to hear." That was a lie. I was totally eavesdropping, but I wouldn't tell him that.

"I swear. Will you two ever get along?" Rhett chimed in, and Bella's eyebrows shot up, her gaze landing on me again.

Don't make eye contact. Don't make eye contact. Don't make eye contact.

I had to get through one more hour of this hell, and then I could escape. Now I understood why Kyle wanted to be left alone.

Jackson

I PROBABLY DIDN'T HAVE a right to be pissed, but I was. She promised that things wouldn't be difficult or awkward with our families. But what hurt even more was the reminder that she truly didn't want anyone to know about us and that she had no interest in me unless I was fucking her senseless.

I didn't expect her to stand up and announce it to her family at the dinner table, but after two weeks, I hoped she might be opening up to the idea. I wanted to tell Rhett first when the time came, take my punch, and promise to tread lightly. I wasn't an idiot. I knew all the reasons why dating my best friend's sister might be a bad idea. But if Ashley and I agreed that was what we wanted, she was worth the fallout.

Grabbing at the back of my neck, I snuck a glance at Ashley. She was wound up tight, her back ramrod straight and shoulders tense like she carried the weight of the fucking world, but I loved how she let herself go when we were alone. That was what kept drawing me back, seeing the serious Ashley lose it and succumb to the pleasure I could give her. It wasn't just when we were having sex either. She laughed and smiled, let her walls down around me, like she was comfortable being herself.

Shit, maybe I was just fooling myself. I had to be prepared to walk away after Christmas if that was what she wanted. I refused to beg her to stay with me. Casually or otherwise.

"Bro," Rhett said, elbowing me in the arm. "I wanted to talk to you about something. Step outside for a minute?"

"Uh—sure."

Fuck. Hopefully it wasn't an *I know what you're doing and I'm going to beat your ass* type of talk.

We excused ourselves, and I followed Rhett outside and down toward the water. Both this house and my house sat on the lake. I would never get sick of these views.

When Rhett ran his hand through his hair more than once and still hadn't said a word, I couldn't take it anymore.

"Dude, what is it?"

"Bella's pregnant."

I almost laughed at the tone of his voice. Like he had no clue how that happened.

"Was it not planned or something?"

He whipped his head around, his eyes wide. "What?" He looked even more confused than he sounded. "Why would you say that?"

"You just sounded—you know what? Never mind." I was happy for the dumb fuck. After all they had been through, they deserved this. I clapped him on the back with a loud thump. "Congrats, man. The fam all know?" I nodded back toward the house.

"Nah, we want to make sure everything's good first."

"Does Bella know you're telling me?"

"Huh? You think she'd want to?"

"No—I mean, does she know you're telling people?"

"I just said we weren't telling anyone." He sounded exasperated, like I was the one who wasn't making sense.

"Rhett. *Why* are you telling me?" My patience was dwindling.

"I want to bring Ashley into the business, have her help manage events with Bella." He ran his hand through his hair and blew out a breath. "Bella will need help after she has the baby. Maybe even before that." He patted my shoulder. "I wanted to give you a heads-up. I know your mom values Ashley, but I'd really like her to be the one we hire for this. Keep it in the family. You know?"

"I do. But I doubt you'll convince your sister. Her passion is the cooking. The Dock caters the events, right?" Did he know his sister *at all*?

Rhett's forehead creased, like this was new information, and I fought back the urge to roll my eyes at him.

"Shit, man. I gotta make this work."

"Offer her good pay for part-time hours—nights and weekends so she can go to school during the day. That might sway her." It was still a crap shoot, but it would give him a better chance. And it could be a good solution if my mom decided to close up the business.

"She wants to go back to school?" He cocked his head to the side and studied me.

I clenched my hands into fists, resisting the impulse to deck him. Yes, he had three sisters to keep up with, not to mention a brother who was struggling both physically and mentally, and now a pregnant wife to dote on. But, Jesus, *talk to your damn sister, dumbass*.

"Yes, and my mom may shut things down in the near future." I glanced sideways at him. "But she hasn't made up her mind on that yet, so keep that between us."

He nodded. "I'll talk to Ashley later this week."

"So then you guys gonna tell her?"

"About what?"

"The pregnancy, dumbass. If you bring up helping Bella with events, you're gonna need to lead with the pregnancy news."

"Oh. Yeah, I'll figure things out with Bella this week and go from there. Sorry, man. I'm just—my head's a bit of a mess." He let out an awkward chuckle.

"Do we need one of *those* talks?"

"What?"

"You know, where we talk about our feelings and shit?" I shot him a smirk as he narrowed his eyes.

"Nah, I'm good." He turned to head back to the house with a huff.

"If you say so." I covered my laugh with a fake cough as I followed him back inside.

Twenty minutes later, I excused myself to leave, thanking Miranda and George for having me. Even though Rhett and I weren't successful in our mission to convince Kyle to join. He told us—quite angrily—that if people didn't leave him the hell alone, he'd move out of this "godforsaken, nosy-ass town." I thought Rhett was going to punch me when I said I was just there for the beer and that I didn't really care if he joined the family for dinner. It made Kyle laugh, though, so in my book, I'd accomplished my mission.

As I walked down the sidewalk, the front door opened and closed quietly behind me. I had no doubt who it was. There was only one member of the Williams family who wouldn't talk openly with me. I didn't stop or turn until I got to my car. I leaned against the side and crossed one ankle over the other, then did the same with my arms.

She stopped a foot in front of me, looking everywhere *but* at me. "Hey."

"I'm up here, princess."

Target hit. Her gaze shot up to meet mine, that sexy temper

already flaring. Good. I was pissed too. Less at her and more at this ridiculous situation. I didn't play games. I wasn't always an open book, especially with the busybodies in this town, but I didn't like hiding either. But this was what I'd agreed to, and I planned to keep my promise. I could give her another week or so, but then she'd have to make a decision. I'd already made mine. I wanted to continue this thing, see where it went. And I didn't want to hide it. Fuck if I didn't want to walk into a restaurant with my hand on the small of her back and let everyone there know she was with me.

"Jackson, I panicked, okay?" She crossed her arms under her chest, pushing her breasts up, her cleavage now more on display. "Eyes up here, *asshole*."

I reached out and dug my fingers into her hip as I pulled her against me, making sure she felt how turned on I was from just a glance at her tits.

Her eyes widened when she felt my cock press against her, her heeled boots putting her almost eye level with me.

"I hate that even when I'm mad at you, I still want you."

"I'm sorry. I didn't mean for it to come out the way it did. Tonight was stressful. I didn't really want to repeat it in four days. And you already confirmed plans with your sister anyway."

I blew out a breath. "I know, and I wouldn't have accepted the invite. But you didn't need to act like I'm not welcome with your family, Ash. You promised that things between us wouldn't affect our friends or families."

"Well—yeah." She blew out a breath and blinked slowly before focusing on my face again.

An irrational fear hit me then. Maybe she was going to end things now that she realized how hard it was to keep this thing a secret.

"You're right. Next time maybe I need something stronger than a glass of wine."

Next time. Like she was willing to do this again at some point. Continue seeing each other even though we'd have to be around her family again. Hopefully not in secret? The encouragement I felt propelled me forward.

"You probably need to know something—" But what the hell was I doing? If she didn't want this to be more than casual, then why even tell her?

Her eyebrows raised, questions swimming in her midnight blue eyes.

"There's a reason my relationships—"

"You mean your flavors of the week, as you so lovingly call them?" Her smirk had me cracking my own smile.

Never did I think that term—a pathetic term I'd once used freely—would come back to bite me in the ass.

"Yeah, those." I ran one hand along the side of my head and across the back of my neck. If there was any hope of her considering a future with me, I needed to lay out my cards. "The two serious relationships I've had ended in disaster. One broke up with me for my college roommate. The other one was using me for my money—she ended things when I stopped buying her everything she wanted. I took that one the hardest. It happened shortly before my accident, and it's why she never showed up at the hospital. After that, I found it was easier to keep things casual."

"Right. Casual makes things less complicated. We have our fun and move on."

Fuck, that wasn't what I meant. I clenched my jaw, working through ways I could tell her that I didn't want things to stay casual between us. That, until now, I hadn't found someone I wanted to spend all my time with and had amazing chemistry with. But before I could speak, the sound of a screaming toddler brought us back to reality.

"I'll call you later," Ashley said before her lips met mine in a chaste kiss. She ran around the other side of the garage, and I made my way around the car.

"I not going!" the little voice screamed. "I stay with Grammy."

"B, if you don't stop, we're not going to the zoo tomorrow." When Rhett used his *dad voice*, it always made me smile.

He was so good with Brendan, even when he had to be stern. He said his head was a mess, but it had *nothing* to do with being a dad to another little one. Me, on the other hand, I wasn't sure I wanted that. Little ones. The older kids at the children's hospital I got. I could spend hours with them. Maybe I would feel different if I found someone who wanted a child of her own.

Did Ashley want kids?

Fuck, I couldn't go there.

Just getting the skittish thing to agree to date me out in the open might prove to be impossible, so there was no point in getting ahead of myself.

I climbed into my car and held my phone to my ear like I was on a call so I'd have an excuse for still sitting in their driveway. Rhett gave me a nod before opening the back door of his truck and buckling Brendan in.

I waited until they drove away before backing out of the driveway and heading home myself.

I wanted nothing more than to see Ashley later tonight, sink inside her, and hold her in my arms. If that happened, the conversation we started earlier might also continue.

But what I kept coming back to was that *she* wasn't ready. *She* wanted to keep this uncomplicated. What she still didn't get was that it was already fucking complicated.

Chapter Nineteen

ASHLEY

I HADN'T SEEN Jackson since Thanksgiving morning when we filled our orders and he left to drop them off. Was it possible to go through sexual withdrawal? Because even though we saw each other Thursday morning, we hadn't had sex since Tuesday, and that was a quickie in my office. Why was the busiest time for catered orders so close to Thanksgiving? Did no one cook?

Now I was at Rhett and Bella's place for brunch. Part of me wondered if they'd figured it out and invited me here for some sort of intervention. But if I knew my idiot of a brother, who was notorious for reacting without thinking, Jackson would've known first.

"More coffee?" Rhett asked as he refilled his own.

"Sure," I said, raising a questioning brow at Bella when he didn't offer to refill Bella's. That was kind of rude.

Bella sank her teeth into her lip and glanced away. There was no way she was already pregnant, right? No one is *that* fertile. They had been quiet since I got here, and after Brendan finished his food, they set him up in the living room with his sippy cup and a show.

"We have news," Bella said, glancing at Rhett, who nodded silently and took his seat. "We're pregnant."

"Wow. That was quick." Holy shit, she *was* fertile. "Congratulations. No one deserves this like you two do." I got up and wrapped Bella in a hug.

After I sat back down, she rambled on about how she'd missed her period but didn't want to get her hopes up and how she thought Rhett was going to faint when she came out of the bathroom with the pregnancy test. Apparently, he was still unfamiliar with how babies were made. I couldn't get a word in, so I sat there nodding my head, feigning interest in every detail. She went on to explain about blood work earlier this week, an upcoming doctor's appointment, and how they hoped to schedule a sonogram for next week. But when she started telling me how they planned to tell the rest of the family, I finally interjected.

"Wait, you haven't told Mom and Dad yet?"

"No, we want to wait until we have a sonogram picture to show them. I just said that." Bella huffed.

"What makes me so special? Why am I the first to know?"

"Technically second," Rhett corrected.

"Wait, who was the first?"

Bella let out a snort and turned to glare at Rhett, and I bit back a laugh.

"I'd rather not get yelled at again. Why don't we change the subject?" Rhett's eyes pleaded with me.

"My *husband* told Jackson at dinner Sunday night," Bella said as she rolled her eyes.

Interesting. I was surprised he hadn't mentioned it to me this week.

"Speaking of Jackson, how's that going?" Bella asked with one eyebrow raised. "You two still at each other's throats, or are things going better?"

I pressed my lips together and studied her. I really wanted to tell her, but I couldn't put her in a situation where she had to lie to Rhett.

"It's going fine. We're getting along." My phone vibrated on the table, and I picked it up to unlock it. The glaring low battery notification was the bane of my existence. I really needed a new fucking phone, but I couldn't help but smile as I read Jackson's text.

> Jackson: Come over tonight. I'll make
> dinner and then make you scream.
>
> Me: Oh? Are we watching a horror movie?
>
> Jackson: Brat.

The sound of a throat clearing across the table brought me back to the conversation.

"Sorry, what were you saying?"

Rhett shook his head. "Bella and I have decided to hire someone to work alongside her at The Dock starting in her third trimester."

"That's probably a good idea." She would need someone to take over for her when she went on maternity leave too.

"We want it to be you."

I looked back and forth between the two of them. "I have a job. That I love."

Bella's shoulders fell. I hated that I was disappointing her, but I didn't want to work for my brother. I'd made that clear five years ago.

Rhett leaned back in his chair. "What if we matched what Barbara pays you? With a more flexible schedule?"

Before I could respond, Bella piped up. "If you wanted to go to culinary school during the day, we could work around your class schedule."

My jaw practically hit the floor. "I—"

I *did not* want to give up the opportunity to actually make food, and I *loved* my job with Barbara. But the prospect of going to culinary school while working part time was tempting. My head was spinning, and I only heard half of Rhett's spiel.

"Take some time and think about it," Rhett said, his chair scraping across the floor as he stood. "We don't plan to seek applicants until after the first of the year, so you have time." He leaned over and kissed Bella's forehead. "I need to get ready for work."

"You *need* to find another closing manager for the weekends," Bella pleaded.

"I know, baby. I'm working on it. Losing an employee just before the holidays isn't ideal."

I spent a little more time with Bella and Brendan after Rhett left for work. But two hours later, I was in my car, heading toward Jackson's.

Jackson

This was not how I saw my afternoon going, not that I was complaining. I sank my teeth into my knuckle as a half-naked Ashley bent over the pool table to line up her shot.

And fuck if a chick who was good at pool didn't turn me on. If I'd known she was this good, though, I might have not been so cocky to wager with clothing. I felt like I'd been hustled, standing there in nothing but my boxer briefs while she was only missing a shirt. Was it wrong that I was hoping she would sink the damn eight ball so I could throw her ass up on the table and give us both what we wanted?

When she had texted that she was leaving Bella and Rhett's, I told her to come straight over. I'd just walked in the door after finishing a lunch order and had needed a shower, so I told her to let herself in. I half expected her to join me, but when I got out and dressed, I found her wandering around my game room.

"Your turn," she said with a smirk. "What am I taking off?"

Shit, she'd missed her shot, and I still had two more stripes to sink.

"We can call it and say you won."

"Nope, I'm enjoying this." She took her time examining me, starting at my bare feet and slowly working her way up to my face.

"I bet you are, you little hustler."

"Not my fault you're cocky and didn't hesitate to take my wager." She shrugged.

"You wearing a thong under those jeans?" Her nod made my cock twitch. "Take them off then."

If I missed another shot, I would be playing in my birthday suit, but it would be worth it to watch her ass as she tried to pocket the eight ball.

Fifteen minutes later, we were both completely naked, and I was slamming hard into her warm, tight pussy. She had her legs wrapped around my hips while I balanced her on the edge of the pool table.

Reaching between us, I strummed her clit, needing her to come. I was too damn close.

She dropped her head back, her mouth open and her breath ragged. "*Fuck*, Jackson. Right there. Harder." A few more moans escaped those parted lips before her whole body shook.

My own release followed, and I swore I saw stars I came so fucking hard.

I rested my head against her shoulder, one arm still locked around her back and the other braced on the table. I brushed my lips tenderly against her collarbone before pulling out of her wet heat.

"Gotta deal with the condom and then I'll start our dinner." I pressed my lips to hers, savoring everything about this girl that made me want things I'd never wanted with anyone else.

Fuck, I was so screwed. Shaking my head, I stepped back and gathered my clothes.

"Go ahead and use the master bathroom. I'll meet you in the kitchen when you're done," I said before leaving the room like it was on fire.

We were both quiet through dinner. I knew where my head was at, but I wondered if she had something weighing on her mind as well.

"You okay?" I finally asked.

She looked up, eyes wide. "Sorry. Rhett and Bella told me about the pregnancy this morning. Apparently, you've known since Sunday."

"Don't give me that look. In one breath, Rhett's telling me, but in the next he's saying they aren't telling anyone. I'm still not sure if I followed that whole conversation correctly."

She laughed, and I shook my head.

"I know what you mean," she said when her laughter subsided. "They want me to come work at The Dock. Did you know that too?"

"Will you be pissed if I say yes?"

Her eyes narrowed. "Yes."

"Then no, I had no clue." I shrugged and let a smirk break out on my face.

She chuckled and rolled her eyes. "You could have given me a heads-up."

"It seemed like a family thing. It wasn't my place. I did tell him you probably wouldn't go for it. That the thing you like the most about your job is working with the food. He was absolutely clueless. You two ever talk? Maybe I listen to my sister ramble about her life too much. How do I get on the Rhett plan for sisters?"

She laughed, covering her full mouth with a hand.

"Can I ask you a question?"

She nodded.

How could I phrase this without being offensive? "You, um, laugh with me, have fun... but you don't really around your family. You're more—" Fuck. If I call her uptight, she'll definitely storm out of here.

"Uptight? Resting bitch face? Stressed?" she finished for me, and now it was my turn to throw my head back and laugh. "Sometimes they drain me. I love them and enjoy my time with them, but they're a needy bunch. With you? I don't know—I feel like I can be myself." She shrugged and looked away like the admission was painful.

Would she run if I told her that she was the first girl in almost six years—possibly more—I could open up to and be myself with? She made it so easy for me to talk about myself, something that didn't come easy for me.

"I get that." I didn't want to spook her but wondered if I

could give her a nudge in my direction. Setting my fork down, I leaned back in my chair. "You gonna stay tonight?"

She tucked her hair behind her ear, and I had to bite back a groan. The handful of times we'd spent the night together hadn't been planned—they'd just happened because one of us had fallen asleep. What would she do if she had to make the decision?

"Do you want me to? I don't have to. I can go home."

"Ash, I want you to stay."

She nodded. "Okay, I'll stay. But I *need* to go to church tomorrow."

I was grinning like an idiot, but I didn't care. "We'll set the alarm, and I'll make you come and feed you breakfast before we need to leave."

She blushed. Ashley Williams just fucking blushed.

Chapter Twenty

ASHLEY

"HERE YOU GO," Dani said, setting two cups of coffee on the table in front of us. "Sophia was so excited when I told her you were stopping by." She reached out and ran her hand over the young girl's head, smoothing the hair away from her face.

Sophia looked up at me wearing a serene expression. Her big green eyes reminded me of Bella's.

When Jackson asked me to come with him to sing at the children's hospital and visit with Sophia and her foster family afterward, I hesitated. The thought excited me, and the last thing I needed to do was get attached to the idea of an us. There wasn't going to be an us. I had to keep reminding myself of that. This was a casual fling. That was all either of us wanted. But when we were in the car together and he reached out to hold my hand while he drove and my stomach did some strange tingling thing, my head swam with ideas I had no business having.

That didn't mean I wanted more, right?

No. I wouldn't go down that road again. I didn't trust myself. Besides, there was no way Mr. Playboy would want anything long term.

Sophia had told us about how she wanted to donate her long locks to one of those organizations that used real hair to make wigs for cancer patients. I'd never met someone so brave and selfless in all my life. She'd kept her hair through all her treatments, even if it had thinned a little, and now how she wanted to cut it all off to donate it? Damn. She had guts.

"I need a haircut too. Why don't we go together? If it's okay with Dani"—I continued when Dani nodded—"and I'll see if I have enough to donate as well."

I glanced over at Jackson when he choked on his coffee, and his eyes were as big as saucers.

I shrugged. "It's just hair. It'll grow back."

When Sophia's face lit up with joy, I was even more resolute.

"That would be so cool!"

"Then it's a date. I'll figure out the details with Dani before we leave."

The weather was mild for early December. We sat comfortably on the back porch in sweatshirts and I wasn't ready for the temperatures to drop, but it was coming whether I wanted it to or not. I prayed we didn't get the snow and ice they were calling for this weekend. I had Victoria's large Christmas party scheduled and I didn't want to have to deal with crappy road conditions.

My breath caught when Jackson's hand landed on my thigh and squeezed. When I looked at him, he was wearing that intense expression—brow furrowed, eyes dark—that made me feel like he could see into my soul. But the look was filled with admiration. My cheeks went hot, and when he chuckled and shook his head, I looked away.

I sat there a little while later with Dani, watching Jackson and Sophia toss a ball back and forth in the backyard.

"He's a good man," Dani said, breaking the silence. "I'm glad he found a strong woman like you."

Oh. Did she think...?

"We're not—" Crap, what do I say? We're just screwing? "We're just friends."

Her eyes widened before she grinned and looked back to where Sophia had just thrown the ball to Jackson. "From where I'm sitting, it's easy to see you two are *anything* but just friends. And if I were you, I wouldn't let that man go. I have a feeling he would do just about anything for the woman he loves."

"He doesn't—we're not—" I could feel heat creeping up my neck again.

"Mm-hmm." She hid her smile behind her coffee cup, but her eyes danced.

I took a deep breath and held it. Was it obvious that we were into each other? We *both* agreed to keep things casual and simple. Neither of us wanted anything more.

But once we were in the car, I couldn't stop replaying the conversation in my head. And when he grabbed my hand, I closed my eyes and swallowed over the lump in my throat.

I was an idiot yet again, and this time, I had no one to blame but myself.

Jackson

. . .

I COULDN'T WAIT to walk into a restaurant with Ashley's hand in mine. I kissed her knuckles as I maneuvered in and out of traffic through the city. It took a little convincing on my part, but she'd finally agreed to go to dinner with me after we left Dani's. I planned to take her to my favorite Italian restaurant. The food was kick-ass, and she would appreciate it.

"I love this song." Ashley broke the silence, turning up the radio and singing along.

"I think I'm rubbing off on you," I said, glancing at the dash, noting the name of the song. "Just Drive" had more of a pop feel than I usually liked, but it had a nice beat.

I pulled up in front of the restaurant and handed the keys to the valet before meeting Ashley on the sidewalk. I grabbed her hand, but she pulled back, then froze. Every line of her face was full of apprehension as she swiveled her head from me to the upscale restaurant and back again.

Shit, was she having second thoughts?

I pulled her to the side of the front door and slid my hand along her jaw. The Christmas lights that wrapped around the bare trees lining the streets illuminated her face.

"Ash, what is it?"

Please don't tell me you've changed your mind.

"When we agreed to grab food—I expected Applebee's. But—*this*." She waved dramatically. "*This* is too much. I—You hate when women expect you to buy them things. I don't want you to think I need this—"

My lips crashed against hers, my tongue tracing them, begging for entrance. When she softened in my arms and gave in to my demanding kiss, I pulled her closer.

"*You* didn't ask," I reminded her when I pulled away. "This is what *I* want." I searched her face as she glanced back at the restaurant. "Come on. It's not like I can't afford it." I grinned.

"Well, then you're paying, because I can't even afford a drink here." She huffed.

I was trying to take the pressure off—make it not such a big deal—but fuck, I should have told her the truth. Told her she's worth *all of this*.

"Fine, I'll pay this time. You can buy at Applebee's next month." I froze. Would she freak out about the idea of being together after New Year's?

She chuckled.

I let out the breath I'd been holding. Maybe she was finally coming around to the idea of us being more.

I pulled her toward the entrance without taking my eyes off her. She consumed me more every day, and that scared the hell out of me. She'd always gotten under my skin. But now she was burrowed so deep that if she really wanted to end this, I was sure I'd never feel whole again.

Chapter Twenty-One

JACKSON

I TWIRLED the low-ball glass of dark liquid in my fingers as I sat at the bar, waiting for Ashley to call. I glanced up, looking out the large windows that lined the back of The Dock. Worry crept up my spine as sleet hurtled toward the ground. She should've called me thirty minutes ago.

Things between us had shifted over the past week. After our visit with Sophia and our date, I had been sure things were moving in the way I wanted them to. Sometimes it was hard to get a read on her, though. I swore she was pulling away yesterday, but then she was my normal hellcat in bed last night. So hell if I knew anymore. Maybe she was purposely not calling me tonight.

Fuck, I'm losing my touch.

"What's going on?" Rhett asked as he sat on the stool next to me. "You look worried."

How much could I divulge without giving my indiscretion away?

My mouth was dry, and I swallowed before taking a sip of my whiskey, needing the burn in my throat.

"Your sister hasn't called yet and isn't picking up her phone. She was supposed to call when she left the Myers' home. That should have been thirty minutes ago."

"Why would she call? Isn't Miguel with her?"

"No, he's home with a stomach bug, and this was a small event. I asked her to call so I could meet her at the office to help her unload."

I didn't plan on telling him I promised to give her one of my "mind-blowing orgasms" once we unloaded the van.

"Myers? Up on the mountain, right? Farther than my cabin?" Rhett's tone held a hint of worry too as he glanced out at the sleet coming down.

I nodded and swallowed down my concerns. That fucking road was the same damn road I'd totaled my car on. It was dangerous even in the best conditions.

"I'm going to drive up. Make sure the van didn't break down or something." I didn't want to voice the worst-case scenario because even the thought made my stomach turn. I wouldn't forgive myself if she got hurt. I should've forced her to let me take this event tonight or at least let me go with her.

"Let's take my truck. Your little toy isn't going to cut it in this weather, that's for damn sure."

"Yeah, okay."

Once in the truck, my nerves intensified. It wasn't only thoughts of Ashley hurt or stranded; I hated to be on this side of the car. After my accident, I felt less anxious in cars when I was in control, not that it had helped when I was the one driving on this damn road seven years ago.

171

I gripped the back of my neck tightly and shifted in the seat as Rhett's truck slid for the third time, but he got control of it easily. I was fucking glad I'd listened to him. His four-wheel drive vehicle handled the road conditions better than my rear-wheel drive Aston Martin.

I really need to buy a damn truck.

"What the fuck is wrong with you?" His glare said I was two seconds away from being dropped off on the side of the road. "Dude, chill out."

"I'm just worried about Ash."

"About my stubborn-ass, never-needs-help sister?" He huffed in disbelief, like the idea had never crossed his mind. But he was full of shit. He was just as worried as me. "Wait—" He whipped his head to me and then back to the road. "Is there something going on with you two?"

"What? *No.*" I ran my hand over the back of my neck but let it fall when Rhett's eyebrows raised in question. It wasn't that I didn't want to tell him. But I couldn't until Ashley was ready. We needed to be on the same page before that conversation happened. "You know our moms will kill me if anything happens to her. I should have just done this party myself, but she's so damn stubborn. That won't stop people from blaming me, though."

"And *why* didn't you just do it?"

"We've been working well together. I didn't want to rock the boat—you know how she can be."

Rhett responded with a grunt of agreement.

Ashley

. . .

JACKSON WAS GOING to kill me. That was if I didn't freeze to death first. And honestly, that thought didn't feel like an overreaction at this point.

I still had a quarter tank of gas. Someone would come along before I ran out, right? I was kicking myself for not replacing my phone months ago; it had been worse lately, and now it wouldn't even power on when plugged into the charger.

Shit. And when Jackson found out, he probably wouldn't do that thing with his tongue that I love. He hadn't wanted me to go by myself tonight because of the impending weather.

At least I was in the van and had heat. I had gotten halfway down the mountain before I slid off the road into icy mud, and I couldn't get unstuck. If Jackson were with me, he probably could have pushed from behind while I hit the gas and freed us. But I had needed space from him today. I'd already let myself get too close; it was time to resurrect some walls.

I had chosen to be stubborn over sensible. Story of my life. And everything was hitting me at once lately. Barbara's scheduled surgery had been moved up, and Kyle was still struggling. Then this thing with Jackson that was confusing the fuck out of me. The job offer from Rhett and the possibility of going to culinary school were weighing on me too. And now this? I was stranded on the side of the road with no way to call for help. What else could possibly go wrong? Maybe my apartment could burn down. That would be the topper to this shit cake.

I slammed my palm against the steering wheel.

Fuck, that hurt. In through my nose, out through my mouth. I'm fine. It's fine. I've got this.

Headlights shone in through the windshield, and I brought my hand up to shield my eyes.

Luckily, the sleet had let up. I climbed out of the van, half relieved and half freaking out when Rhett and Jackson got out of the truck.

I watched as worry faded from Jackson's face and was replaced with relief as he moved in my direction. I wanted him to wrap his arms around me, but stupid Rhett was here. Jackson's heated stare warmed me even without his embrace. Three steps from me, his hand twitched like he wanted to reach out, and I froze. As much as I wanted him to touch me, he couldn't, and he knew it. Evidenced by the way his jaw clenched.

"What happened?" Rhett asked, looking at the van and paying no attention to us at all. Hell, Jackson probably could have hugged me and Rhett would have missed it.

I gestured to the vehicle before saying, "Oh, I stopped to take in the stars—what the fuck do you think happened? I slid off the road. The front tire is stuck."

"Why the hell didn't you call?"

I winced at the hurt in Jackson's expression. He thought I wouldn't call him? I met his eyes, silently pleading with him to understand that he would have been my first call.

"My phone won't turn on." The second the words were out of my mouth, Jackson's glare softened. His hand twitched toward me again before he fisted it. I wished I could cover it with mine to show him I understood.

Rhett just laughed. "Didn't Bella and I tell you to deal with that two weeks ago? You need to be more responsible about this shit."

Jackson's glare shot to Rhett and his hand twitched again. This time, I didn't think he was reaching for me, though. Odd, I would have thought Jackson would join in on the scolding. He, too, had been telling me for weeks to get a new one.

"Yes, Mr. Know-it-all." I crossed my arms and frowned.

Obviously, I should have done it by now, but I hated the whole process. "I'll go tomorrow."

"Good," they said in unison.

I rolled my eyes. I was well aware that I was an idiot.

"Can we get the van unstuck, or do you feel the need to condemn my bad decisions a little longer?" I asked Rhett.

They looked at each other before walking around the other side of the van. I couldn't hear their conversation, but I swear *frustrating* and *brat* were thrown out there.

"It's a good thing I installed the winch on the front of my truck a few months ago."

"Yeah," Jackson agreed, two steps behind him, but all his intensity was focused on me. He blew out a breath and ran his hand down his face. I had a strange urge to go give him a hug just then, like he needed one more than I did.

I shook my head.

"Pushing isn't getting this beast unstuck. Ash, get back in. Jackson, help me get it hooked up."

With one quick glance at Jackson, who had straightened his shoulders and seemed to have moved past his issues, I got back in the van and rolled the window down.

Rhett climbed into his truck while Jackson stood off to the side of the van in front of me, looking at me before giving me the sign to move forward.

"Give it some gas, princess," he yelled loudly after a moment.

"I am." But I was hesitant. The roads were slippery and the last thing I needed was to fall farther into the ditch or worse, flip the van.

But it's fine. I'm fine. I got this.

I pressed harder on the pedal, and the engine roared.

"More. And turn the wheel to the right."

I didn't see how that would help, but I did as instructed. The wheels skidded, and the van teetered closer to the edge of

175

the ditch. I pulled my foot off the pedal and spun the wheel to center.

"No, stop!" Jackson yelled after I already had. "You're going to flip the fucking van into the ditch."

"You're the one who said right." I glared.

"Not your right—my right. Turn it to my right!"

My face heated, even though the mistake had been his, not mine.

"How was I supposed to know that?" I sighed.

"I know, I know," he ranted. "I'm just *frustrated.*" He called something out to Rhett before turning back to me. "Give it gas and turn the wheel to the left. *Your* left."

"Are you sure this time?" I teased.

Jackson huffed, but the tiniest smirk pulled at his lips.

Rhett stuck his head out his window. "Can't you two get along for five minutes? I'd like to get home to my wife sometime tonight."

I rolled my eyes, but I was thankful Rhett was the one who had come with Jackson tonight. With the tension this high, anyone else would have noticed something going on between us. But I wanted to get home as much as Rhett did, so I pushed on the gas and turned the wheel to the *left* when Jackson gave me the go-ahead. Finally, the van lurched forward, and a second later, it was back on the road.

"Thank you!" I yelled out the window.

Rhett gave me a nod as the two of them unhooked the van from Rhett's truck. I breathed out a sigh of relief before Jackson came to the window and tipped his chin, motioning for me to get out, but once I did, I wished I hadn't.

"I'm driving," Jackson declared with a look that said *don't argue*.

Normally, he realized that shit wouldn't work on me, but his demand had me putting my hands on my hips and winding up for an argument.

"Ash, just let him drive. The roads could still be slippery."

I whirled on my brother, who'd been an overbearing idiot since he got here. "Oh? And a little girl can't handle it?"

"Clearly not," Rhett muttered, gesturing to the van. "You should have let Jackson do this event, or at the very least, you should have had him go with you."

I crossed my arms, ready to yell. The fucking nerve. I opened my mouth but snapped it shut when I saw Jackson's face.

Shit.

It hit me then. His accident had happened on this road. The one he still struggled to be on, even on the clearest days and especially when he wasn't the driver. Yet he'd gotten in the passenger seat of Rhett's truck to come get me.

I swallowed hard, and Jackson turned away. Rhett was probably oblivious to the way Jackson still felt about his accident.

"Fine, we'll do the whole big man can drive car while little woman needs caring for."

Jackson spun back to me, his mouth open, probably ready to correct me, but he stopped the second his eyes met mine. This time, it was my arm that twitched. And Jackson didn't miss it.

"Great. Try not to kill each other." Rhett chuckled.

Once Rhett drove off and we were on our way back down the mountain, I finally spoke.

"This would have gone better if you hadn't brought Rhett."

"I know—but he was the one with the truck," he said, white knuckling the steering wheel. "I don't know if I want to hug you, kiss you, or spank your ass."

I couldn't help but smile. "I'm not sure that would be much of a punishment."

"What am I going to do with you?" He shook his head.

Part of me wanted to tell him I wasn't kidding. The idea of him spanking me sent a jolt straight to my core.

"Where are we going?" I asked when he turned left instead of right on Main Street.

"My house. You can drive me to my car in the morning and take the van back to prep for your brunch then."

"What if I don't want to do that?"

His jaw clenched, and he didn't turn to look at me. *Shit*, I was just messing with him.

"Then I'll take you back to your car," he said, his words barely audible between gritted teeth. He'd adopted the broody asshole tone, the one I couldn't decide whether I hated or found sexy.

"Do I still get that orgasm you promised me, and possibly the spanking to go with it?"

I'd never actually tried that before, but the thought of him plowing into me from behind while slapping my ass did something funny to me. But more so, I wanted to lessen the tension that was sucking the air dry.

He finally turned and looked at me with that cocky smirk I loved to hate, and his eyes were so intent on me I couldn't help but squirm.

"You can have whatever you want tonight. I'm just happy you're okay." He reached over and laced our fingers together. "You had me worried."

And my insides turned to mush.

"Aw, you care," I cooed.

"More than I'd like to," he mumbled.

I wasn't quite sure how to dissect that, but I could totally relate.

Chapter Twenty-Two

ASHLEY

I DROPPED Jackson off at his car the next morning and almost got caught kissing him in The Dock parking lot. Now I was alone in the catering kitchen prepping for today's event and the other order we had scheduled. I'd promised Jackson that I would go straight to the phone store after I was done. He probably doubted me as much as I did.

Would it really hurt to be unplugged for a few days?

After another hour, I had everything packaged up and helped Kelly and Miguel load up. Kelly would be overseeing a small business luncheon today—she had stepped up to run smaller events lately—and I would deliver the order for the baby shower.

I was almost through cleaning up when the back door opened and Jackson strolled into the kitchen.

"I got something for you, princess," he said, holding up a familiar-looking bag.

"Please tell me there isn't a phone in there." I crossed my arms over my chest, narrowing my eyes.

"There totally is a phone in here. It's an updated version of the one you had."

He smiled like he'd just cured cancer or something.

I raised one eyebrow at him. Was he serious?

I could buy my own damn phone, for god's sake. What if I wanted a different model or style?

I knew that the women he was used to dating—no, not dating; fucking—the women he usually fucked liked spending his money and having him buy them shit. But that sure as hell wasn't me.

"Jackson, you can't *buy* me a phone."

"Too late. Just say thank you and don't make this into something it's not." He widened his stance and crossed his arms over his chest.

"You're the one making it into something. You're acting like my sugar daddy. I'm not like all those other women."

I knew the moment the words left my mouth that I shouldn't have said them. The way his body went taut and his jaw clenched told me all I needed to know.

"If that's what you think, how you think I see you, then we need to end this *now*."

I pinched my eyes closed and swallowed over the thickness that gathered in my throat.

"I know that's not how you *see* me." But was that true? *Did I know that?* I wanted to scream out, *then how* do *you see me?* But I was a coward, and I didn't. "I'm sorry; I just meant that's how it makes me feel."

"Because I bought you a goddamn phone that you needed? So next time you're in trouble, you have a way to call for help? Because I care about you, even though you make me *fucking* batshit crazy?"

I couldn't help but smile. That made two of us. We stood there for what felt like an eternity. A battle of wills. Neither willing to back down. But finally I knew I should cave; I felt it in my soul. Like he *needed* to do this. And I *needed* to be okay with it or he would walk away. And I wasn't ready for that.

Something told me this was a catalyst, provoking a change that was necessary, but one I didn't understand.

"It's really the newest model?"

His eyes narrowed, suspicion written all over his face. "Yes."

I walked toward him and wrapped my fingers around the bag's handle. *Easy there, boy. Don't bite.* Stretching up on my tiptoes, I pressed my lips to his while he stood stock still. He didn't kiss me back. *Fuck*. Had I really messed this up?

"Thank you," I mumbled, staring at his chest.

A gasp left me when he grabbed me by the waist and drew me into him, burying his nose in my hair.

"You're so fucking frustrating. Anyone ever tell you that?"

"You do. All the time."

He chuckled before pulling back to look down at me. "I know you're different. You'd prefer the basics over the luxuries any day. And even when you want a high-end pair of shoes, you'll settle for knockoffs." He caressed my cheek and brushed my hair away from my face, tucking it behind my ear. "You're used to being on your own and taking care of yourself. I get that. But every now and then, let people do small things for you. And it's okay to splurge on yourself sometimes."

His tone was so sincere. But what almost knocked me off my feet was how well he understood me. For a moment I wished things were different. That we weren't who we were.

I nodded, at a loss for what to say, and stepped out of his embrace. "I need to deliver this order."

"Want me to do the delivery while you stay here and switch your phone over?"

I smiled. "Better yet, I'll do the delivery—you stay here and switch my phone. I have no clue what I'm doing. It's part of the reason I avoid the process."

I set the bag on the counter and fished my old phone from my purse.

"It should be as simple as transferring the SIM card and grabbing your stuff from the cloud," he said, like I knew what the hell he was talking about.

"A what card? And the what?" I shrugged and batted my lashes dramatically.

He laughed. "You really are a horrible actress. I have faith you could figure it out if you wanted to, but I'll stay and do it for you."

"Thank you. And Jackson, could we... I mean, I know..." I shuffled on my feet, feeling nervous all of a sudden.

"Spit it out, Ash."

I looked up into dark brown eyes that searched my face. "I know you don't usually put up a tree, but I think you should this year. Right in front of those windows that line your great room."

"Only if you go with me to pick one out and decorate it with me. We can do it tonight."

"Um, okay... you sure?"

He shrugged. "Yeah, why not? I don't usually have a reason to put one up. But if you want to, then I have a reason."

I must have stared at him for a beat too long because he raised one eyebrow at me. I didn't know how to take his *whatever you want* reaction to me half the time. My ex did that a lot, and most of the time he did it just to shut me up, never following through those promises. But in the last two months, I'd learned that Jackson always followed through.

Once in the car, I fought back the strange feeling behind my eyes. Like that twinge in my sinuses that said I might cry? Yeah, that one. I didn't cry. And I wouldn't start now. But the emotions and realizations hitting me were big.

I *was* ready for more. I wanted more. Maybe it couldn't be with Jackson, but I wanted someone—no, I *deserved* someone who would treat me like he did. Who could see who I was. Who saw my worth.

After so many years and so many dates that I didn't let go anywhere, being with Jackson for the last few weeks had shown me how amazing it could be.

Holy shit.

Was I *finally* ready to open myself up to that again?

Later that night, I lay naked in his strong arms. He was such a bear of a man. I always felt so small like this, but at the same time, he made me feel safe and cherished. The Christmas lights glowed and twinkled in the darkened room as I shimmied deeper into his embrace. After we picked up a tree and spent the evening decorating it, we'd ended up on the sofa in his great room, desperate for each other once again. I ran my finger over the tattoo on the inside of his right forearm—the one symbolic of New York—tracing the Central Park gate and the outline of the Brooklyn Bridge.

"Sleep, Ash," Jackson rumbled against the top of my head.

"Yes, sir," I whispered back with a chuckle.

"Hmm, I like the sound of that."

I bet he did. I closed my eyes and drifted off, content to fall asleep every night just like this.

Chapter Twenty-Three

ASHLEY

Sitting in a salon chair next to Sophia a couple of days later, I stared at our shoulder-length cuts in the mirror.

"I love it," she said, swishing her hair from one side to the other.

I ran my fingers through my hair, taking in the weightlessness, feeling almost unrecognizable

"I do too. It's so much lighter."

The stylists held up matching ponytails so we could pose for a picture. Sophia donated two inches more than I did. I barely made the minimum cut off.

Will Jackson like the shorter hair?

Not that I should really care what he thought. But I did.

"Do you think Jackson will recognize us?" Sophia asked with a giggle.

I laughed. "I hope so."

Once we were out on the sidewalk, I pulled out my phone and texted Jackson that we were on our way.

"Ready to check out the Museum of Science?" I asked as I kept stride with Sophia's excited skip. She had been illness free for almost a month now.

"So excited!" Sophia nodded.

We continued our trek until Jackson came into view. I raised my hand, waving, and his smile grew when he saw us.

"Look at you two with matching haircuts."

"Do you like it?" Sophia chirped.

"I do." He brushed his fingers through my short locks. "You both look beautiful."

His eyes met mine, and my breath lodged in my throat at the desire that swam in those dark chocolate orbs.

Sophia walked ahead of us as we made our way through the museum, stopping occasionally to check out the hands-on exhibits. Jackson rested a palm on the small of my back as we stood off to the side while Sophia watched a live presentation I'd completely tuned out. Science wasn't really my thing.

When his arm snaked around to rest on my hip, I leaned into him.

"What do you really think of my hair?" I asked, turning to face him.

"I like it short. It suits you. But then again, I've always thought that."

"What do you mean? I think I've only had it this short twice, maybe? Once when I was a teenager and then again the year I came home from college."

"Yup. And both times I thought you looked sexy as hell." He coughed to cover a laugh. "In fact, Caden gave me shit when I tried to hide a semi from Rhett when you were hanging around in a bikini that summer you came home from college. I cursed my damn swim trunks that day."

185

I stared at him like he had completely lost his mind. Had he really found me attractive all this time, and I never realized it? He raised one eyebrow at me and then winked. Like he freaking knew he was making waves.

But when he leaned over and nipped at the shell of my ear, I had to squeeze my thighs together to relieve the tension gathering there.

After the museum, we grabbed food and meandered through the light displays downtown before dropping Sophia off at home. I must have fallen asleep in the car on the way to Half Moon Lake, only waking briefly when a pair of thick arms picked me up and cradled me against a warm, solid chest.

It felt like a dream, but I think I asked if I could stay in his sexy arms forever.

Chapter Twenty-Four

JACKSON

WHEN I WOKE the next morning, reaching out for Ashley's warm body, she was gone. Each and every night spent together had led to waking up and getting inside her. She was a morning sex person.

After propping up on my elbow and scanning the room for her, I glanced at my smart watch to check the time, finding a text notification waiting for me.

Ash: Left early. Didn't want to wake you.

WHAT THE FUCK? Last night she'd told me she wanted to stay in my arms forever, and now she'd hightailed it away from me? While I was asleep? I had a serious case of vertigo from the emotional tennis match she was playing.

If I had to guess, it had finally hit her that she wanted more, but in the light of day, she'd gotten spooked. Again, one step forward and two steps back.

Patience. You're playing the long game.

An hour later, I was sitting in the passenger seat of Rhett's truck, heading to do some Christmas shopping. Rhett had the day off, so he was taking Brendan to pick out gifts for Bella. He called and asked if I wanted to tag along. I didn't have a good excuse to say no, and I still had people on my list to shop for, so there I was.

"Uncle Jackson!" Brendan exclaimed from the back seat.

"Hey, buddy," I said, turning around and sticking my fist out for a bump.

"Thanks for tagging along." Rhett glanced sideways at me. "Figured navigating crowded stores with a two-year-old might be easier with help."

I nodded. Rhett had his hands full, that was for sure. But spending the day with Ashley and Sophia yesterday had made me want that life more and more. The problem was that I wanted that *with* Ashley and Sophia, and I was starting to doubt whether either was attainable.

"What are your parents feeding you? You're growing like a weed." I teased Brendan as he leaped into my arms once I'd unbuckled his car seat.

"Mama say weeds are bad."

I laughed. This kid cracked me up.

Our first stop was to a jewelry store where Rhett wanted to put together one of those charm bracelets with beads and such for Bella.

"You know Bella's gonna cry when you give her this, right?" I asked as Rhett chose the last charm to put on it.

"Bella will probably cry no matter what I give her." Rhett chuckled.

Would Ashley like something like that? I shook my head at the thought. I should stick to something *not* sentimental, or I'd risk spooking her again.

But you know who *would* love this idea?

"Do you have smaller sizes?" I asked the saleswoman, boosting Brendan higher on my arm while he squirmed to get down.

Rhett took over with Brendan as I chose charms to go on the bracelet.

"Any change with the situation with Sophia?" Rhett asked as he sat next to me while the woman wrapped our purchases.

"Nah. She's finally healthy, though, so she's moving in the right direction—hasn't been sick since the beginning of November, and she's doing good at Dani's for now."

Rhett nodded. "So you've seen her recently?"

"Yeah, she and Ashley got their hair cut together yesterday."

Fuck. Why did I say that?

Rhett paused, raising one eyebrow at me.

"I didn't realize Ashley knew Sophia." Rhett's questioning stare had me shifting in my seat.

No big deal. Tell him the truth without telling him the whole truth, right?

"Yeah, I told her about the children's hospital and Sophia back in October, and she was interested in volunteering. So she's gone with me to visit once or twice since then and really connected with Sophia." I paused and glanced at Rhett. Nothing in his gaze said he was suspicious, but there was a curiosity there, so I continued. "Sophia wanted to get her hair cut so she could donate it to an organization that makes wigs for kids. I think Ashley realized that she was nervous, so she offered to do it with her."

"My sister? Has been volunteering and spending time at the children's hospital, and then cut off all her hair to support a ten-year-old girl she just met?"

The surprise in his voice had me locking my jaw. I wanted to tell him that Ashley was one of the most selfless people I knew, remind him who had taken care of everyone *but* herself the week they'd gotten the news about Kyle. But I kept my mouth shut. Maybe one day I could stand up for her the way she deserved. But for now, I had to keep my promise to her or I would ruin any chance I had.

I shrugged, ready to change the subject. "What's the deal with this adoption celebration this weekend?" Maybe it was a guy thing, or just a me thing, but I didn't get why we needed a party to celebrate Rhett becoming Brendan's dad on paper. He already was in all the ways that mattered.

But I'd be there to support them regardless. With everything they'd been through, maybe celebrating the simple things made them feel more grateful for where they were.

"Just a small gathering at The Dock. We'll finalize it at a hearing next week, but we wanted to celebrate with our friends and family."

"Bella's idea?"

"Of course."

I slapped Rhett on the back and chuckled. He would walk over hot coals for that woman. But I guess I could relate these days.

Chapter Twenty-Five

ASHLEY

I CAME BACK to my apartment feeling restless. So I cleaned. The floors, the kitchen, the bathroom. I organized my clothes and shoes. And cleaned out my refrigerator. Then I took a shower, did my hair—the much shorter style would take some getting used to—and put makeup on. I had a meeting with Jackson's mom at the office that afternoon. Excitement rolled through me. Maybe we'd finally have the conversation where she would ask me to take over the day-to-day running of things.

A ping from my phone brought me out of my thoughts. I grabbed it off the counter and opened the message thread with my sister.

Hattie: Still good to meet for lunch?

Me: yep. Mamacita's?

Hattie: Chips, salsa, and margaritas? Count
me in.

Almost an hour later, I sat across from Hattie. I froze with a chip midway to my mouth as she tilted her head, her eyes slightly narrowed.

"What?" I asked, instinctively patting my hair to check for bird shit or something. Her look said something was amiss.

"I just can't believe you cut your hair," Hattie said as she brushed her hair over her shoulder. Her natural color was a dark chocolate brown, but she'd been putting highlights in her hair for years.

"I needed a change." I shrugged and popped the chip into my mouth.

"You look like Savannah now."

"That's a stretch. I don't have pink streaks, and I don't have a nose ring either."

"You missed it the other day. Dad had a few choice words to say about that one."

"I bet he had *a lot* to say on the matter."

I thought Savannah had moved past the trying to find herself phase when she went back to her natural color over the summer. But then she showed up last week with pink hair and the piercing. Even though she could pull it off and I thought the nose ring was kind of cool, my youngest sibling was still a bit lost. She always joked that she was adopted because she didn't have that need to be still and settle down like we all did. And not in the traditional sense—the marriage and kids—but Hattie, Rhett, and I had always strived to plant roots. Build something we could call our own.

Kyle and Savannah were more similar than they realized, although they dealt with their wanderlust differently. Kyle's military career satisfied his need to do something bigger than himself and not be stuck in one place. Were some of his issues now because he felt confined to this small town again?

"By the way, Matt said you still owe him that drink some-time," Hattie said with a smirk. "He's a really nice guy. You should give him a chance. I think you'd really hit it off."

Matt, one of the newest bartenders at The Dock, had asked me out twice since he started working there this summer, and months ago I told him I would grab a drink with him sometime. But then everything went down with Jackson, and I had brushed Matt off the last time I saw him. He did seem like a nice guy. Maybe I should consider going out with him after the new year.

But the thought had my stomach churning.

Hattie's voice brought me back to the moment. "Or not— I think he's hot, but the look on your face says you don't agree."

"It's not that. He is attractive. I—" Before I could finish that thought, my phone screen lit up on the table. Jackson's name appeared, and I quickly dismissed it. I picked up my menu and pretended to study it to hide my blazing cheeks. I felt rather than saw Hattie's intense scrutiny. Jackson and I worked together, so with any luck, she wouldn't read too much into it.

"Okay. Spill. What's going on?"

Shit. What the hell? Did I have *secret* stamped on my forehead?

"What do you mean? We're ordering lunch, aren't we?"

Hattie huffed. "Don't change the subject. You have *never* ordered anything but the enchiladas here, so why are you looking at the menu?"

"Am I not allowed to see if they have anything new?"

"Fine. Keep your secret. It'll eventually eat you alive, but whatever. I'll be here when you're ready."

That was Hattie. Calm but direct. She wouldn't push. But damn, did I feel like revealing my truth to her. Besides Bella, Hattie was the one I confided in the most.

Once we ordered our food, I chewed my lip, silently debating with myself about telling her *everything*. But I kept coming back to why. What was the point? Things with Jackson would be over in a few weeks.

I had tuned out Hattie's rambling, so when she asked, "what do you think?" I had no clue what she was talking about.

"Sorry, what?"

She tilted her head and studied me. And the words left my mouth before I could stop them.

"I slept with Jackson."

Hattie's eyes widened and her mouth dropped open, forming a perfect *O*. "You did what?" She leaned forward, and her voiced dropped to just above a whisper. "Jackson, Jackson? Like our brother's best friend and the guy you hate? That Jackson?"

Her questions were unnecessary; she knew who I was talking about. But I nodded anyway.

After a moment, she finally said, "Like a one-time thing? Or—"

I shook my head. "Like an almost every night, sometimes during the day, sometimes multiple times a day thing."

"Oh my."

"There's more," I admitted when she didn't say anything else.

She put both elbows on the table and leaned even closer. "I'm still digesting the first part."

"I don't want to stop."

She laughed. "Um, okay. I'm still confused about how we got here. But if Jackson is what you want, tell Rhett and do you. He'll get over it."

I shook my head vigorously.

"Why not?" Her forehead creased.

"I don't want anyone to know," I whisper-yelled.

I was making absolutely no sense, and I knew it.

"I think the ship has sailed on that, sweetie," she said, pointing back and forth between us.

I huffed out an exasperated breath. "I don't want *everyone* to know." I tucked my hair behind my ear before revealing more. "It's—temporary. Not serious. So we're not telling anyone." Crap. He asked me to let him tell Rhett before I told anyone else. "Shit," I mumbled.

"What?"

"He asked me to let him tell Rhett first—"

"Wait. You lost me. He wants to tell Rhett?"

"Yup. He got all weird and made me promise that I'd let him talk to Rhett before anyone else. But this isn't what he meant. You have to promise to keep this to yourself."

"Hmm." Her eyes narrowed on me, and I had the urge to squirm. She reminded me of Mom in that moment. "Ash, it sounds like this is more than casual sex. There's no way Jackson would be willing to tell Rhett if it wasn't."

I shook my head. She was wrong. "Jackson doesn't do *more*. You know his *flavor of the week* thing."

"I actually can't remember the last one of those, can you?"

"Well… there was that one in May… or was it June? And then—" Did he bring anyone around over the summer? I couldn't recall.

"Okay. And?" One perfectly shaped brow arched as she watched me quietly. After what felt like an eternity, she sighed. "I think that's an excuse you're hanging on to. But humor me. *If* things were different, could you see yourself dating him?"

"*If* things were different, yes. But things aren't different. We agreed to *just* sex. But I think he helped me realize something."

Hattie crossed her arms and sat back in her seat. "Which is?"

"I'm ready to try again. Find someone who makes me feel valued and respected."

"Jackson makes you feel like that?"

I looked out the front windows of the restaurant, watching people walk down Main Street.

I swallowed over the lump in my throat. The truth lodged there.

"Have you told him that?" she asked when I didn't respond.

I closed my eyes for a long moment, readying myself to ask why she was pushing this, but she continued on.

"You watched Bella and Rhett avoid telling each other how they felt for years because they *assumed* neither wanted the same. So I'm just saying it wouldn't hurt to tell him that you want to continue seeing him. Worse case, he says he doesn't, and you walk away."

The thought of the humiliation and rejection that could cause was enough to turn me off to that suggestion. But in a way, she was right. I could only blame myself if I wasn't honest. Jackson knew my history, though. If he wanted more, he would talk to me. Wouldn't he? He wasn't the type of guy to hold back. If anything, he was too forthcoming with his opinions, good or bad. But I liked that about him; I never had to wonder what he was thinking.

"I'll think about it. In the meantime, you have to *promise* not to tell a soul. If Savannah gets wind of this shit, the whole town will know in minutes."

She laughed, knowing just how true that statement was. Not only had I made that promise to Jackson about letting him handle Rhett, but I also wanted to be on the same page if anyone else was going to know. If he told someone and the news spread all over town, I'd be pissed. Guilt washed over me.

I shouldn't have told Hattie, but I trusted her to keep my secret.

Once in the car, I considered calling Jackson back, but instead typed up a text.

> Me: Sorry. Was at lunch with Hattie.
> Heading to the office for a meeting with
> your mom.

Three little dots appeared and then disappeared multiple times before I put my phone away and drove to the office. Before going in, I checked to see if he had responded yet.

> Jackson: Ok. Come over afterward?

I chewed on my red fingernail. Did I want to go to his place tonight and ride him until my legs burned? Of course. Should I? Probably not. Really, what I needed to do was shit or get off the pot. That was the stupid-ass saying, right? Put my big girl panties on and see if he wanted to continue past our expiration date. My stupid hormones won the debate minutes later as I shot back a final text.

> Me: Only if you'll make dinner and do that
> thing I like.

> Jackson: hahaha. I do many things you like.
> You'll need to be more specific. But deal.
> Dinner and all the things you like. It's a plan.

I rolled my eyes at his cockiness as I climbed out of the car.

But he was right. I did, in fact, like *all* the things he did. And I wasn't just referring to the sexual things. I was so screwed.

Chapter Twenty-Six

JACKSON

Dinner was in the oven. We usually made dinner together, so her request had been a surprise.

I checked my watch again. It had been more than two hours since her text. How long was she planning to stay at the office?

I had a lasagna baking and a bottle of wine chilling. We could put together salads when she got here. Actually, scratch that. After I made her come with my mouth, then we could finish up dinner together. I should spank her ass for sneaking out this morning before our usual morning ritual.

My front door slammed, and when I stepped into the foyer, I was met with blazing blue eyes. Directed at me. *Shit*.

"You *fucking* asshole," Ashley spat out as she slammed her hands on her hips.

What? Why was I an asshole? I mean, I was, but what warranted the name-calling?

"Care to explain, princess? How did we go from do *all* the things you like to I'm an asshole?"

"You knew. You knew I was going to lose the only thing I've cared about for the last five years. You fucking knew!"

Shit. Fuck. Dammit.

"Ash, take a breath." Jesus, Mom. It could have waited until after the holidays. "It wasn't my place. It's not my business, and when we talked about it last, she wasn't even sure."

"Don't. That's a load of bullshit and you know it."

I closed the space between us and reached out for her, but she stepped away.

"I hate you," she seethed.

Her words were full of anger, but we both knew her lips were lying.

"No, you don't." I took a step closer, and she took one back.

"I do. I hate you. So much." Her voice cracked as she held back tears.

I inched forward as she stepped back.

"You're mad, hurt, probably sad. And you can't take it out on my mom, so I'm the easiest target. I'm okay with you taking your aggression out on me." I glanced over her shoulder, eyeing the distance to the wall as we continued our dance. If I could just—

"You're delusional if you think—" Her words died when her back hit the wall.

I caged her in with my arms and lined my body up with hers, effectively pinning her to the wall. Her eyes blazed with a combination of heat and rage.

"You have two choices, princess. One, you can yell and scream at me, tell me how much you hate me. Then I can fuck you rough and fast against the wall. Or we skip the first part, go straight to the fucking part, and then have a calm conversation afterward."

"Or I can just leave."

"You can. But I don't think you will. The rational Ash I know is there, under the hurt and the outrage."

"I'm so mad at you." Her hands landed on my chest as if she was ready to push me away.

"I know." I angled closer, letting my breath skate across her jaw. "Let me make it better."

Her exasperated sigh and the way she tilted her head, exposing her neck to me, was all I needed to know she was caving. I nipped at the skin below her ear and was rewarded with a mewl.

Pulling back, I met her gaze. And this time, she fisted her hands in my shirt instead of pushing me away. I crashed my mouth against hers before she changed her mind.

I let her dig her nails in and pull on my hair as hard as she wanted while I fucked her against the wall. Every time I tried to control a kiss, she bit down on my lower lip. She drew blood at least once, but I didn't care. Soothing her hurt was all that mattered.

She probably felt betrayed, like I should have had her back. Done something. Said something. And maybe I should have.

I smirked when she screamed, "I hate you. I hate you for making this feel so fucking good."

"You don't hate me." I nipped at her ear. "Now be a good girl and come for me."

"Damn you to hell" were the last words she uttered before coming apart in my arms.

I can't handle it if she walks away tonight and *please don't let this be our last time* were my final thoughts before following her over the edge.

I had to make this right somehow. If she let me explain, I'd make her understand.

Ashley

WE WERE breathless as we sat on the floor next to each other with our backs against the wall. The wall he'd just had me pinned to. Neither of us had said anything since we'd come together in the most intense and primal way I'd ever experienced. We were mostly clothed. My blouse was open at the top, and I was pretty sure one of us was sitting on my underwear. And even though my anger had receded in the last several minutes, I still wanted to punch him.

"Fuck, Ash. I *never* forget." He scrubbed a hand down his face. "I got caught up in the moment. All I could think of was you and making you not hate me..."

What was he rambling on about? What did he forget?

"I don't hate you. But I'm still mad at you." I bumped his shoulder with mine and gave him a half smile, but the fear etched on his face had me worried. "What's wrong? What did you forget?"

"A condom, Ash. We didn't use protection."

"Shit," I mumbled before blowing out a breath. "I have an IUD, so birth control isn't a problem. But... when's the last time you were tested? With your revolving door of women, I'm assuming you go regularly..."

He glowered at me, and I chuckled. I meant it as a dig, but I wasn't wrong.

"There you go making assumptions about me again. I thought we were past all that."

"We were until your mom told me you knew about her plan to close up shop. So now we're back to me *assuming* you're a selfish bastard."

He huffed and leaned his head back against the wall. "I'm clean. Got tested over the summer and have *only* been with *you* since May."

I tried, unsuccessfully, to swallow the gasp that rose in my throat. I searched his face for signs of dishonesty but didn't find any. My conversation with Hattie came to mind. *Shit.* Was I blind to who he'd been lately?

"I'm good too," I choked out.

He nodded, and we sat there for a moment before he shifted and lifted his hand with my lacy thong dangling from his fingers.

"Missing something, princess?"

I swiped at it, but he pulled it out of my reach before I could grab hold of it. Hitting his hard-as-fuck stomach muscles did nothing but make him chuckle. I arched my eyebrows as he tucked the piece of fabric into his shirt pocket.

"Seriously?"

"Yup. I want to eat dinner knowing you're wearing nothing under that skirt."

"Who says I'm staying for dinner?"

"*Me.* I made lasagna. And I still need to do that thing you like."

I was trying really hard to stay mad at him. But I also wanted lasagna and his head between my legs.

"I'll stay for dinner, but I'm not staying the night."

His face fell into a frown before he schooled his features and nodded. Then he got to his feet, moving toward the oven that was now beeping. He wanted me to stay, and I could make an excuse, tell him I hadn't brought anything with me to stay over, but he would see right through that. I'd stayed before without packing a bag. Truthfully, I just needed some space to think after today.

"Want to make salads?" he asked without turning to look at me.

"Sure." I busied myself cutting vegetables. The conversation with his mom kept weighing on my mind, running on a loop. I had until the first of April to find another job. I didn't want another fucking job. I wanted the one thing I'd worked so hard for.

"Do you want to talk about it?" Jackson's voice came from behind me.

I glanced over my shoulder to find him leaning against the counter, arms crossed. "What am I going to do? You of all people know how much I love my job. The choices in this small town are practically nonexistent, and if I did find something, none of them would be in the food industry."

"I think you should take this opportunity to go to culinary school."

The knife clanged against the counter as I dropped it and spun to face him.

"Why do you keep harping on that? I know you're used to getting your way, but just because that's what *you* think I should do doesn't mean that's what I want."

He closed his eyes, and I zeroed in on the slight tick of his jaw before his gaze locked on me again.

"Why are you so stubborn?" He pushed off the counter and came to stand in front of me. "I see *you*. Your worth. Your talent. I'm not going to apologize for encouraging you to do something I know you want but are too damn scared to do."

I wasn't going to do this with him. I refused to go there again, refused to feel like I had to explain myself. So instead, I asked another question that had been bothering me.

"How long have you known? Huh, Jackson? Maybe that's what you should be apologizing for. Did you know the first time you fucked me? Or when I confided in you about my plans for the business?"

I bit the inside of my cheek and closed my eyes. I would not cry in front of him. I hadn't cried about this yet, and I sure as hell wasn't going to do it now. I'd hold my shit together until I was alone. I was fine. Everything would be fine.

Two large hands cupped my face, and warm lips pressed a kiss to my forehead. His thumb swiped along my lower lip as his mouth feathered against mine.

"Look at me," he muttered.

I blinked my eyes open once I was sure I could keep the tears at bay. "Don't feed me your bullshit, Jackson."

"I wouldn't dare." He smirked, and I had the urge to slap that grin off his face. But I didn't. "My parents told me about a month ago. The day we hooked up the second time." His grip was firm, holding me in place, almost like he was worried I would pull away. "But Ash, you need to understand that at the time, it was just something they were considering. If I'd known she was going to spring this on you today, I would have mentioned it or asked her to let me talk to you first."

I wanted to believe what he was saying. But did it matter? Why were we wasting our time? In less than a month, we would go our separate ways. We'd go back to being Rhett's sister and Rhett's best friend. Nothing more.

Jackson wasn't my boyfriend, and he had no obligation to tell me anything. And I didn't need to cause unnecessary drama. We would enjoy the next couple of weeks and then end things like we'd planned all along.

I managed a nod and pulled out of his hold. Something flashed across his face, like he wanted to say more, but the impassive mask came back into place just as quickly.

That was the moment the chasm between us got bigger. Yeah, we both knew this was the beginning of the end.

Chapter Twenty-Seven

JACKSON

I WAS confident my plan would work. After Ashley left my place Tuesday night, I was done with the constant walls she put up. I'd apologized for the way everything went down, and I really hated that I hadn't handled things differently, but I couldn't force her to accept my apology or even believe that I was sincere. I had to make it right and show her I wanted her to do what made her happy.

I drew up the proposal and confirmed that Rhett and his dad were on board. We would meet next week to go over everything in more detail. It took a little finesse to come up with a believable reason for investing *my* money in expanding *his* business. But I hadn't lied. My mom had an extensive client list, and without Callahan's Classic Events, they would have to seek out another catering business. So why not invest my money in Rhett's business and encourage Ashley to transfer the clients to *her* family's business? It was a solid business expansion plan.

Tonight, we were all gathered at The Dock where we were celebrating Rhett's adoption of Brendan. I cuffed and rolled the sleeves of my button-down as I walked away from Rhett and the conversation about our plans that had the stupid-ass grin plastered on my face. Maybe once I told Ashley, she would let those walls down, see I truly cared. And maybe she'd be open to the idea of us continuing to explore the possibility of a relationship.

I stopped in my tracks as my eyes latched on to Ashley. She wore a flirtatious smile and was leaning on the bar, talking to the new bartender.

When the asshole moved in so their faces were only inches apart, a cocky smirk on his face, I almost lost it. But I kept my feet planted and my fists balled at my sides.

Savannah's voice brought me back to the moment. "Hey, hot stuff. You ready to rock my world yet?"

I tried to keep the mask of indifference in place, but she reared back like she didn't recognize me. So I forced a smile. Rhett's youngest sibling usually made me laugh. Her lack of filter and no-fucks-to-give attitude were comical.

Hattie walked up, handing a pink-colored drink to Savannah.

"Who's the asshole behind the bar?" I meant for it to come off as nonchalant, but I could hear the bite in my tone.

Hattie's gaze swung that way. She didn't answer my question but brought her drink to her mouth and sipped while trying, unsuccessfully, to hide her smile.

"Matt? He's our newest bartender and, by the looks of it, Ash's newest boy toy." Savannah cocked her head, taking in the scene at the bar. "Lucky bitch."

"Savannah," Hattie scolded as she slapped her arm.

"What? Just because Ashley is quieter about her hookups than me doesn't make them less real. We both enjoy the opposite sex, just mostly in the bedroom. Nothing wrong with that. Men are annoying, and neither of us has time for that."

"Okay, shut up now," Hattie hissed out between gritted teeth. She looked at me then, her eyes filled with apology.

Did she know about us? Was Ashley really done with us and moving on to her next casual hookup? Maybe Hattie knew all this and was told to keep her mouth shut.

There was no fucking way I got sucked into this again. Another woman who just wanted what I could give them in the bedroom or out of my wallet? There was no way I read Ashley *that* wrong, was there?

Well, screw that. It was time to find out. Now.

"Look what you did," Hattie whispered.

But I didn't stop to question her meaning. Just marched in the direction of the only person I could see at the moment.

As I came up behind Ashley, Matt's words were like a punch to the gut.

"I get off in an hour. We could grab those drinks after we're both done here."

The words left my mouth without clear thought. "Sorry, she's busy," I snapped out.

Yeah, I was an asshole. But the only thing I could see was the imaginary sign above her head that flashed *mine*.

Ashley spun at my words, her eyes wide, pleading with me not to make a scene.

Too late.

"I know I'm not anything special, but you're coming back to my place tonight." In my head, it sounded less like a demand than the way it actually left my mouth. But fuck it. I didn't give a shit at that moment.

Ashley glanced behind me, her eyes wide. Usually, they

reminded me of a calm, beautiful morning at sea. But now? They looked like the start of an ominous storm.

"You better be something special if you're taking my sister back to your place."

I pinched my eyes closed and locked my jaw.

Fuck me.

"Rhett—" Ashley started.

But he interrupted, his pissed-off expression still locked on me when I turned to face him. "Outside, now," he gritted out as he turned and walked out the front doors.

"Look man, I—" I'd barely come to a stop in front of him before his fist slammed into my jaw.

I'd give him that one, but if he tried that shit again, I was laying his ass out.

"Please tell me you're not fucking my sister!"

Was this a punch me first and then ask questions situation? He'd been my best friend for fifteen years. One would think that he would know it was more than *just* fucking. In his defense, though, that was exactly how it started. But I wouldn't tell him that.

I deserved his punch for that. For lying. For so many reasons.

"Isn't it obvious?" I mumbled as I raised my gaze to his shocked expression. Guess he wasn't prepared for me to admit it. I'd already lied so many times. Why would he expect me to be truthful now? But that was all the truth he was getting from me if he planned to stand there and jump to conclusions.

"You asshole," Ashley's words rang out from the front steps of The Dock.

I knew in that moment we were over. I had lost the girl and my best friend all in one night.

Chapter Twenty-Eight

ASHLEY

I COULDN'T BELIEVE HIM. Did he not fucking trust me? I was trying nicely to end the conversation with Matt and get away from the bar. And I sure as hell wouldn't have said yes to grabbing drinks with him. But no, Jackson had to interfere and all but piss on me. *Jesus*. Possessive and controlling, and we weren't even *together*.

And now. Now. He told Rhett that we'd been *fucking*. Nice. Real nice.

Rhett took one step forward, and Jackson matched it, perhaps to punch him right back.

"Stop. Both of you," I said. The last thing I needed was my brother getting into a fight on such a special night for his family. Bella would never forgive me. "Jackson, you need to leave."

"Ash, listen—"

"No. There's nothing else to say. We've always had an expiration date. It's just ending a little sooner than planned. It's best we stop this charade now before it causes any more damage."

Maybe if we ended this now, we could salvage some of the destruction we'd both caused.

"Charade? Is that all this was?"

"You're the one who just said we were *only* fucking," I challenged.

"That's not what I said, and it sure as fuck wasn't what I meant!"

I took a deep breath in and held it, struggling to keep my emotions in check and steady, then let it out slowly. I could break down tonight in the privacy of my bathtub with a glass of wine. I wasn't doing it here in front of my family and half the town.

Jackson took a few steps forward, but Rhett pushed him back.

"Just go. You're not welcome here now," Rhett spat.

I felt momentarily guilty as hurt and anger crossed Jackson's normally expressionless face.

This was what I'd hoped to avoid. I should have never let this happen.

Jackson stood still, eyes intent on me, like he expected me to disagree. I couldn't. I needed him to leave. We needed distance, and fast, before my whole family was out here weighing in on our situation.

The mask came back down in place as Jackson gave a stiff nod and turned toward his car.

My legs felt like they were going to give out, but I stayed strong and stood firm.

Once Jackson sped out of the parking lot, I breathed out a

sigh of relief that was immediately replaced with tension as Rhett rounded on me.

"Don't," I said with a hand up, cutting off whatever he was going to say. "I don't need your lecture or your scolding right now. I get that you're pissed, but let's get through this night, and then you can yell at me tomorrow."

Rhett brushed past me without a word, and I stood there for what felt like hours until a door shut behind me and an arm wrapped around my shoulders.

Hattie pulled me into her side as I lay my head on her shoulder.

"How did this night go so wrong?"

She was silent, but I could hear the judgment anyway.

"Because you didn't talk to him."

I tried pulling out of her grip, but she tightened her hold before going on.

"Ash, you and Jackson have been playing with fire, and you were bound to get burned. You had to see this coming. Eventually, this was going to blow up."

"Thanks for the lecture, *Mom*." I yanked out of her hold and turned, but she gripped my forearm before I could walk away.

"I'm not giving you a lecture—but it's clear Jackson has feelings for you. You realize that now, don't you?"

"I—" I honestly wasn't sure what I knew anymore.

"Like those stupid big kind that make men do dumb things," Hattie finished.

My cheeks went hot. "What would make you think that? Huh? 'Cause from where I was standing tonight, it looked like he pissed on me like I was his property and then told Rhett we were *fucking*. Not dating. Not together. Not anything but fucking."

The hurt on his face before he walked away flashed across my mind, causing my throat to tighten. I needed a strong drink. Maybe two. Anything that would help me forget and not feel. I stomped past Hattie but froze at her next words.

"Be prepared. Almost everyone in there has caught on."

I'm going to kill him. Or go into hiding.

I hadn't decided which. I couldn't take the looks of pity and whispers again. But I squared my shoulders and walked back inside.

I'd dealt with this crap once before. I could do it again.

Chapter Twenty-Nine

JACKSON

I COVERED my head with a pillow, hoping the constant pounding would stop. For the love of god, it needed to stop. Finally, it was quiet again. I removed the pillow from my face and closed my eyes. My smart watch vibrated, and because it was second nature, I glanced at it.

> Rhett: Answer the goddamn door. I know
> you're in there. Your fancy little toy is in the
> drive.

I should have known. I'd avoided his phone calls for the last few hours. But I had nothing to say to him. Yes, I fucked his sister. Broke bro code rule number one. He had a right to be pissed. But so did I. I figured once he found out, I'd take my punch, and he'd eventually slap me on the back and give his approval. He'd known me long enough to know I wouldn't have gone there unless I was serious about her. In the end, I had no one to blame but myself. There were so many things I could've—should've—done differently, and now it was too late.

The pounding started again. Fuck. He wasn't leaving until I opened the door. I threw my legs over the side of the sofa in my office in a huff and cursed to myself all the way down the stairs.

Once in the foyer, I swung the door open. "What the fuck do you want?"

"What the fuck do I want? We had a meeting this morning. You didn't show up or pick up my calls. My *wife* has been chirping in my ear for days, saying I overstepped and there has to be more to all this and *I* need to fix it. Even though I have no idea what *I'm* supposed to fix. And dude, *why* do you look like shit? When's the last time you showered? What the *fuck* is going on?"

Was he joking? Did he honestly expect me to invest in his business after he told me I was no longer welcome there? Sometimes Rhett was so dense it was scary.

I crossed my arms. "I assumed since I wasn't welcome there, that meant my money too."

"The expansion wasn't *my* idea, if you remember correctly. *Bella* thinks you wanted to do it *for* Ashley. I figured if that was true, you would've shown up today." Rhett ran his hand through his hair before going on. "Or since you guys aren't, you know, anymore, you don't want to do it."

"*Fucking,* Rhett. That's the word that got us all into this mess. Remember?"

His eyes narrowed. "Is that what it was, Jackson? Was it *just* fucking?"

"I'm not doing this. Go home, Rhett."

I felt a moment of satisfaction when I slammed the door

in his face. But I deflated when his voice came from the other side.

"I'm not leaving."

Ugh. I hate this motherfucker right now.

I swung the door open again and turned, moving straight for the kitchen as I heard Rhett's footsteps behind me.

"If you insist on staying and being a pain in my ass, at least let me get a cup of coffee."

He sat, eerily silent, at my kitchen island. His head tilted, staring past me. I followed his line of sight and wished I hadn't. It hurt to look at, but I couldn't bring myself to erase it.

My Samsung smart refrigerator's memo app was open with a note on the front.

Sorry—used your last pumpkin spice coffee pod. See you tonight.

Not sure why she'd apologized. She had to know I only kept them stocked for her. It was another punch to the gut, knowing I didn't need to buy any more pumpkin spice coffee pods.

"You're usually the one who wants to talk about his feelings like a fucking woman, so let's do that." He pointed to the refrigerator. "That is *not* just fucking. One, you don't drink pumpkin spice coffee, and two, you rarely let the chicks you sleep with stay the night."

I shrugged. "What's your point, Rhett?" I waved in the direction of the half bath off the kitchen. "Go look in the fucking mirror and tell yourself that, 'cause I already know it. At least for me it was more."

"What the hell, man?" Rhett threw his arms up like I was the problem. "Why didn't you say any of that?"

"I shouldn't have had to. You should have gotten there by yourself. You should have *known* I would never touch one of your sisters if I wasn't serious." I slammed my coffee cup down. "And Ashley knows as well as I do that we weren't just fucking. I have tried and tried to break down those impenetrable walls. I failed. She had a choice to make in that moment, and she made it. Nothing I can do about that."

"Other than sit here and wallow in self-pity?"

"I'm not wallowing."

Rhett shook his head. "Look, man, you're right. I'm... I'm sorry. I overreacted as usual."

"Yeah, you probably should work on that overreacting thing before baby number two comes along."

He laughed. "Yeah, probably."

"Want a cup of coffee?"

"You do realize it's past noon, right?"

"Well, it's morning for me."

"Not sleeping well?" He smirked.

"Shut the hell up."

I couldn't seem to get the smell of her out of my house. And no matter what room I walked into, reminders of her jumped out at me. We'd had sex in almost every room. I'd found I could only get a few hours of sleep in one of the guest rooms or my office.

"So you don't want to move forward with the expansion, then?"

I scrubbed a hand down my face and picked up my coffee mug. "I don't fucking know. I'm pissed at her. That she didn't choose us. Me. But god dammit, I want her to be fucking happy."

Rhett chuckled. "Love'll do that."

I almost choked on my coffee. No one said anything about love.

"I didn't say—"

"Now who's being the dumbass?"

Fuck. Did I love Ashley? I really enjoyed the sex. Like more than with anyone else I'd been with. And I wanted her to be happy, feel supported, cherished. I wanted to support her successes, and I'd been willing to do whatever it took to help her. I enjoyed spending time with her and wasn't ready for things between us to end. She got me in ways not many people did. It was easy to be myself and open up, let her in. But...

"I—" The words to deny it wouldn't come out.

It was impossible, though, wasn't it? I'd always found her attractive. But how could I have fallen in love with her? I could barely stand to be in the same room as her a few months ago.

"Uh huh..." Rhett's shit-eating grin had me shaking my head.

Maybe the dumbass was right. But she didn't love me back. If she did, she wouldn't have been so quick to give up on us.

"Yeah, I love your pain in the ass, stubborn sister. But that doesn't change anything, does it?"

"It's a long game, man." Rhett shook his head. "Remember how long I had to be there for Bella before she would even consider giving me a second chance? Bella said Ashley was miserable when she talked to her yesterday. So maybe there's still hope."

Maybe. But I wasn't the type to believe in the impossible.

Chapter Thirty

ASHLEY

EVERYTHING I'D WANTED WAS FALLING into place. So why did I feel so miserable?

I was still in shock from what Rhett had just told me. And part of me felt like he was holding something back. I loved the idea of running the off-site catering for The Dock, and with the expansion plans, I'd have a small kitchen and lobby area to make my own. I suggested bringing Kelly on board full time as an events manager to help Bella *and* me oversee on- and off-site events.

I didn't want to push, but I'd love it if we could bring Miguel in too. Both Kelly and Miguel had been loyal and hardworking employees. But we still had a lot to figure out over the next six months, plus the construction would take time. I would help Barbara with the remaining events after the new year and prepare to launch the catering side of things at The Dock, which would leave me with quite a bit of extra time. Time I could devote to something I was finally ready to admit I wanted.

I was looking into taking culinary classes early next year. I wished I could say I was happy Jackson wasn't around to give me that knowing smirk of his when he gloated.

That was a lie, though.

I missed him. I missed *us* something terrible. Yeah, I screwed up, but so did he. We should've had a conversation, just the two of us. Not in front of the bartender, my family, and half the town. I should've spoken up instead of letting him walk away, but I took the easy way out, allowing myself to hide behind my walls.

I still wasn't convinced he wanted the same thing I did, and I couldn't go back to casual, so where did that leave us?

Bella and Hattie had spent the better part of the last week trying to get me to talk about it. Trying to get me to talk to him. But seriously, what was the point? What we had, or could have had, wasn't fixable.

As I entered the main dining room from the back offices of The Dock, I blew out a breath and spotted my mom covering all the tables with linens as Hattie followed behind her, adding centerpieces.

We hosted a Christmas party at The Dock every year. It was a family tradition, and I was nervous about the possibility of seeing Jackson for the first time since it all went to hell. I knew we probably needed to talk. If only to hash things out.

I stepped up next to my mom, grabbing one side of the linen she was putting on a table to straighten it.

"What do you want me to do?"

She planted both hands on her hips and narrowed her eyes. *What did I do*? I was rarely on this side of my mother's glare. I glanced over her shoulder to Hattie, who refused to make eye contact and all but ran to the other side of the restaurant. What the hell was going on?

"I have something to say. I need you to listen." My mom softened her stance, sending me a small smile. "You're allowed your privacy. I have always respected that. But I need you to hear something, and then I'll butt out—It's time to start trusting your heart again."

"Mom." I sighed. She meant well, but... "You don't really know what happened."

"I know enough."

I wanted to kill my siblings. What happened to having each other's backs?

"Savannah?" But as soon as the words were out of my mouth, I knew better. Hattie had just run away.

"Ha. She would tell the whole town before she told me anything."

"I can't believe Hattie told you. Did you bribe her with pie?"

"Of course. Hattie *and* Bella, to be exact. You know they can't resist my pies." She laughed before her lips formed a thin line. "But it didn't take much for them to spill either, 'cause they seem to think you're purposely sabotaging what you could have."

"I don't know, Mom. What if—" I swallowed over the thickness in my throat. Not able to give words to the one thing that had always stopped me from committing to someone else.

"What is it, baby girl?" She reached out, placing her hand on my cheek, and I leaned into her touch.

"What if I miss all the red flags again? What if he doesn't want me? What if... What if I get my heart broken?"

"And what if he's the *one*?" She sighed. "You gave your heart to someone once who never cherished it. But you're a different person now, and as scary as it sounds, you need to trust in love again."

She pulled me into a hug, and I embraced her comfort as her words played on repeat in my head.

What if he's the one?

I STOOD AT A HIGH-TOP TABLE, looking out over the main dining room when we'd finished setting up. Tables and chairs with beautiful lantern centerpieces lined the two walls of windows, and the middle stayed open for dancing. A decorated Christmas tree sat in one corner, and lights and garland lined the bar top that faced the dining room.

I smoothed my clammy hands down the sides of my black and red dress as Bella joined me.

"I can't believe you and Hattie sold me out to Mom."

"In my defense, she'd already pieced most of it together." She shrugged. "I think she just wanted us to confirm parts of it. She baked three of our favorite pies. And then supplied us with hot chocolate. I can't even resist that combination when *not* pregnant."

I rolled my eyes and huffed.

Bella smiled and nodded over my shoulder. "Jackson just walked in."

I turned, taking in the tailored suit that hugged every muscle I knew he had. His wide shoulders and thick thighs always did me in. And those freaking tattoos hidden beneath that mesmerized me.

But he wasn't mine to ogle anymore. He never really had been. When I raised my eyes to his, it was almost my undoing. But what actually broke me was when he yanked his gaze away and turned to talk to my father.

Luckily, my father seemed to be mostly in the dark about what went down between Jackson and me. My siblings could all be jerks sometimes. Selling me to out to Mom was one thing, but Dad? That would've been a crime.

Savannah had unnecessarily apologized to me for her part in all the drama. She didn't know. And what I kept coming back to was that the blame fell solely on me.

Hattie was right. Secrets had a way of coming out. And Jackson would probably say he knew this was a bad idea from the start.

"I can't believe he came," I said, following his movements.

"He has to sign papers since he's a silent investor now. But I think *you* are the real reason he showed up tonight." Bella said it so nonchalantly that I almost missed her meaning.

"He's *what*?" My voice raised an octave on the last word, causing a few people to turn in my direction.

"Do you really think it was all about sex for Jackson? He approached Rhett with the expansion plans the day *before* the adoption celebration. But again, what do I know?" Bella shrugged. "Rhett and I went around and around our feelings for each other for years, never having the courage to address them. We're the idiots. You and Jackson couldn't possibly be that stupid, right?"

I placed my hands on my hips and narrowed my eyes. "Trying to get me to talk about it the normal way didn't work, and sending Mom after me hasn't either, so what? You're going to try reverse psychology?"

"Whatever will get you to open your eyes and see what you guys had was special."

I rolled my eyes. The truth of the matter was that Hattie and Bella were both right. There was more between us than amazing sex, I was sure of it. But a bit of doubt still lingered; I couldn't align the Jackson I'd known for so long with the one who treated me like I hung the freaking moon.

And could I actually open my heart to him? Conquer my fear of being hurt again? That was my biggest issue at the moment.

And the question still remained: did Jackson actually want

more? He might have felt the same connection developing between us, but that didn't mean he would be willing to embrace a serious relationship with me. Especially after the way I'd hurt him.

My thoughts continued to whirl as my gaze landed on Jackson every few minutes.

Had he really done what Bella said? And before the blowup with Rhett? What did that mean? A person doesn't invest hundreds of thousands of dollars in his buddy's business without a really good reason, right? Had he done it *for* me?

And then my mom's words from earlier hit me again. *What if he's the one?*

When he disappeared out onto the back patio, I made my feet move. I had to stop hiding. It was time to be brave.

I wanted more, but did he?

Who was I kidding? Even if there *could be* more, I didn't think Jackson would forgive me. I had been a coward. I hadn't been strong enough to fight for us or admit my feelings.

I took a deep breath before stepping outside. My gaze roamed over his back as he leaned over the railing, staring out at the lake.

"Hey," I said, noticing how his spine went taut with tension.

This was going well already. But I was determined to say my piece. I couldn't live with myself if I didn't at least try.

He turned before leaning back on the railing and crossing his arms. "Hey."

We stared at each other as the courage I had five minutes before faded away. He raised one eyebrow, waiting for the words I was obviously struggling to find.

I didn't know how to start this conversation. Did I just blurt out *I've been a miserable mess this week and miss you like crazy. Please tell me you feel the same*?

The door opened behind me, and I glanced over my shoulder at Hattie as she stepped onto the patio.

"I'm so sorry to interrupt, but Rhett and my dad are ready to sign the papers if you are." She glanced apologetically at me before adding, "Take your time, though."

I turned back to Jackson as he approached. "I still can't believe you did this." I waved to the door Hattie had just gone through.

Jackson shrugged like it was no big deal. "It's just money." He took two steps forward. "I can't fix everything, but I can fix this."

Did he mean us? Did he want to fix us?

"I should go." His gaze didn't leave my face, and he didn't move.

There was so much to say, but I was struggling with where to start.

I blew out a breath, defeat washing over me before nodding.

"Okay," I mumbled, looking down at the deck at our feet.

He brushed past me. "See you around, Ash."

I stayed out there until the chilly December air became too cold before heading back inside. I wasn't in the Christmas spirit or the mood to socialize, but I forced a smile anyway.

"So what happened?" Bella asked as we took a minute between making our rounds.

"We didn't really get to talk." I followed Jackson's movements as he walked out the front doors.

Was he leaving? Already? A sadness I hadn't let myself truly feel washed over me.

"Or did you chicken out?"

"I tried." I pinched my eyes closed. "Well, not really. I'm not sure what to say. I'm not good at this stuff."

"Neither was your brother, but he figured it out, didn't he?" Bella bit her lip. "We both had to figure out how to communicate. You can't let Jackson leave without telling him how you feel."

I didn't respond, just took off, knowing she was right. I hurried through The Dock's dining room toward the front door. But I was too late. My eyes blurred as his car pulled out of the parking lot.

What now?

Chapter Thirty-One

JACKSON

"Fuck," I yelled, slamming my hand into the steering wheel.

Should I turn around and go back? Force Ashley to talk to me and admit she has feelings for me? But I wanted her—no, I *needed* her—to do this of her own accord. I thought she had more to say when we were outside. I gave her an ample opportunity, but she didn't.

Was I making a mistake? I thought giving her time to come to terms with the idea of us was the right thing to do. But now I wasn't sure. Should I have told her I wanted more? Probably.

But creating a scene in front of her family was ultimately what led us here. So I wouldn't do that again. I'd ask her to meet me tomorrow. At the very least, we should clear the air. That decision took a little weight off my shoulders, and I blew out a long breath just as my Bluetooth indicated an incoming text from Ashley. I glanced at the screen of my phone where it was mounted on the dash, hope blooming in my chest.

What the hell? Was that a link? Why the fuck would she send me a link? I pulled off the road and snatched the phone off the dash.

My lips curled up into a smile as I clicked on the song she'd shared with me. Closing my eyes, I listened to the lyrics that filled the car.

Less than ten minutes later, phone in my hand, I pushed through the doors of The Dock, not even slowing down as I spotted my parents, my sister, and her boyfriend waving me down.

Ashley couldn't just send me this and not expect me to do something about it. If this was truly how she felt and if the meaning was what I hoped it was, then we were having this conversation tonight.

I stalked toward her, my gaze intent as I watched her mouth drop open and her eyes go wide.

"Jackson," she whispered.

"What does this mean?" I held up my phone as the song "If I Didn't Love You" played softly.

"I—" She glanced around us, noticing that we were gathering some attention.

I took a deep breath to rein in my need to have this discussion here and now and gave her the choice instead.

"Do you want to go outside and talk?"

"No," she hastily said before adding, "I mean... no, here is fine."

Her words said one thing, but the way her body was rigid with tension and she was wringing her hands meant she was anything but fine. I had to give her credit for not hiding, for pushing through despite how vulnerable she must feel. But I didn't give a damn if she hid from everyone else. I just didn't want her to hide from me.

I smirked. "You sure, princess?"

Her eyes blazed, but this time not from anger at my use of her pet name, but from desire.

She nodded and cleared her throat. "This week has been hard for me. I've missed you. I've missed us." She glanced down, but quickly back up. "The stupid stretching routines in the morning that I hate but enjoy at the same time. Listening to music while we cook. I miss how you make me laugh, how you make everything fun."

"Ash." I took a step forward but stopped when she put her hand up between us.

"Let me finish, please? If I don't say this now, I'm afraid I'll lose the chance." She tucked a piece of hair behind her ear.

I nodded, tracking her movements. Aware of the rise and fall of her chest, the way she hugged herself across her stomach. The vulnerability of it all had me itching to pull her close and tell her all the things I should have said weeks ago. But the truth was that she hadn't been ready to hear them then. I had to allow her to climb this mountain, but I sure as hell would be at the top, waiting for her.

"Jackson, I sent you *that* song because *if* I didn't freaking love you, then this wouldn't be so damn hard. I could go to the grocery store without looking for you or cook a meal without thinking of you. I've barely been able to listen to music because almost every song reminds me of you. The way you love music, especially country, even though you grew up in New York City." She smiled but shook her head. "I've tried to tell myself that I need to move on. Put my walls back up and go back to the way life was before you came crashing into it. But you broke me, Jackson. In the best way. And I don't want to go back to life before you."

Finally, unable to stop myself, I closed the distance between us and reached out, cradling both sides of her face.

"You won't have to, Ash. I don't want a life without you in it either." I captured her mouth and slanted my lips over hers, feeling her relax completely into my embrace. Pulling back, I held her gaze. Now it was my turn. "I'm still not sure how it happened. Most of the time, you drive me crazy, but I fell hard for you. And the lyrics to that song hit close to home for me too. Not being with you this past week was torture."

A single tear trailed down her cheek, and I brushed it away with my thumb. She was crying. Ashley, the toughest woman I knew, was crying. I wasn't sure I had ever seen her cry before that moment. It was only a single tear, but I'd take it.

"I'm sorry, Jackson." She reached up, gripping my wrists as I continued to hold her face in my hands.

I kissed her forehead and then pressed my lips to hers. "I'm sorry too. We both made mistakes. But what matters now is we're working through them. We're being honest and communicating and all that shit that makes a relationship work. Right?"

She chuckled. "Yeah, and all that shit." She pinched her eyes closed before cracking one open. "Is Bella crying?"

I pulled her into my chest, wrapping my arms around her back, and then glanced over her shoulder at the comical scene.

"Yep. And your mom too." My gaze landed on her father, who was glaring in our direction. "Your father, on the other hand, looks like he wants to murder me. Think he'll be okay with this?"

"He'll come around. Rhett did, right?"

I laughed, remembering our conversation earlier in the week. "Yeah, he stopped by, and we had a heart to heart."

She smirked. "Oh, I'm sorry I missed that."

She tilted her head back and stuck her bottom lip out. "Will you stay? Please?"

"Whatever you want, princess."

"I *never* thought I'd be happy to hear you call me a spoiled brat again."

"I want to spoil you, and you can be a brat sometimes. But I can call you baby, or honey, or sweetheart if you'd like."

"I think I'm quite fond of *princess*, actually."

Good, cause so am I.

She took me by surprise when she stepped back out of my embrace and folded her hand into mine, then lead me out onto the small dance floor.

All eyes were on us, but neither of us cared. She was all I saw, and her attention never wavered from me.

I chuckled when I heard Savannah say "lucky bitch" off to my right.

"*Shit*," I mumbled as my mom and Ashley's mom were deep in conversation. "She's gonna be pissed."

Ashley tilted her head and followed my gaze. "You don't think she'll approve?"

"No, she'll be ecstatic. I'm a little worried our moms are gonna start planning our wedding, though." I laughed when her eyes widened. "But she's gonna be disappointed and give me a lecture." I dipped closer, brushing my nose along her jaw.

"We'll probably both get a lecture." She laughed before her lips found mine.

It had been over a week since I'd held her, kissed her, was buried inside her. And we had at least an hour or two of obligatory Christmas party fun to partake in before we could have the privacy I needed to do the things I wanted to.

But when she ran her tongue against the seam of my lips, I almost said *fuck it* and carried her to my car so I could take her home to my bed.

The clearing of a throat brought me back to the present, and I reluctantly pulled away, glancing over my shoulder to Rhett, who'd brought Bella out to the dance floor.

I raised one eyebrow at him as he glowered at me. I thought we were good. What the fuck was his problem now?

"Dude, I thought we were cool," I said over Ashley's shoulder.

Ashley glanced toward him and just rolled her eyes with a huff. "Ignore him."

"I'm coming to terms with the idea of the two of you. But I'm not sure I will ever be cool with you groping my sister's ass with your tongue halfway down her throat."

"So you mean I can't tell you what she likes me to do with my—"

He hastily pulled Bella away from us as he muttered, "Fucking asshole."

I shrugged. "I guess that's a no."

Ashley buried her face in my shoulder, fighting back laughter.

"I love hearing you laugh; I've fucking missed that."

Her head shifted on my shoulder, and she pressed a soft kiss against the side of my neck. I hugged her tighter to me as we moved, not ready to let her go quite yet.

I wouldn't ever let her go. I hoped she knew that now.

Chapter Thirty-Two

ASHLEY

I REALLY WAS A LUCKY BITCH, wasn't I? I was snuggled into Jackson's side with a mug of piping hot chocolate that he'd whipped up for me. He'd added toasted marshmallow creme that was to die for. I smiled then, realizing he knew I liked it that way.

Jackson and I had just gotten home from spending Christmas with his family and then mine. Exhaustion was pulling at me from all sides. I wouldn't be opposed if he wanted to strip me down and have his way with me for the second time today, but I was *so* ready for bed.

"I'm so tired I can barely keep my eyes open."

"Yeah, me too. I'm not sure I even have the energy to get off this couch right now." He leaned over, pressing his lips against my temple. "Next year, we're hosting Christmas here. With both of our families."

I smiled at the idea that this would be *our* home next year.

"Did you think about what I suggested?" he said into the room lit only by the lights of the Christmas tree.

I nodded. "Yes."

"Yes, you've thought about it? Or yes, you'll move in with me?"

I chuckled and glanced up at him. "Jackson, are you sure? You've been used to having your own space for so long. I—"

He captured my mouth in a demanding kiss but pulled away just as quickly. "Woman, you should know by now I never say things I don't mean." He cradled my face in one of his large hands. "I want you here every night. In my arms."

"Okay." I nodded. "My lease isn't up until the end of February, so I'll slowly pack and bring stuff over."

When he had first brought it up a couple of days ago, he told me to take some time to think about it before giving him an answer. I'd waited for all those old fears to rear their ugly heads. Especially since this was happening so fast. But it felt *right*. Like loving him and knowing he loved me. It was more than enough to trust in us.

Getting to know who Jackson really was, a man who looked and acted tough on the outside but who loved hard.

Dani's words when we visited a month ago floated through my head.

He would do just about anything for the woman he loves.

"I can see how that'll go." He shook his head, and I smiled. "You'll wait until the last possible second, and we'll be scrambling to get hundreds of shoes packed up and out of your apartment."

"You're the one who added two more pairs to my collection today." *Authentic* Jimmy Choos and Louboutins.

233

He chuckled, and I settled further into him, resting my head on his shoulder.

"Was it me, or do you feel like we got weird looks from everyone today?" His deep voice was only a whisper, like he, too, was about to drift off at any moment.

"I think they're still getting used to us. We're not at each other's throats for once, and it's throwing them off."

"Maybe..." He shifted and nodded to the tree. "I think you missed a present this morning."

"I did not." I made sure to double-check when I packed up all the gifts we'd taken with us when we left this morning.

"Be a good girl and go check. Before we both fall asleep."

I had something special for him too. I'd hidden it last night after I wrapped it instead of putting it under the tree.

He slapped my ass when I got up, and I narrowed my eyes at him. "Don't start something you can't finish, old man."

"I'm never too tired—and too old, for that matter—to fuck you senseless. So cut the sass and open your gift."

I rolled my eyes but was totally planning to call his bluff. If I didn't fall asleep first.

I dropped to my knees in front of the tree and pulled out the present. It was the size of a medium clothing box. I unwrapped it to find a small, thin jewelry box sitting on top.

"Jackson, it's beautiful," I breathed, taking in the simple Christmas tree charm on a chain.

"There's more."

I set the jewelry box down before unfolding the tissue paper. A shirt? I lifted it up, noticing the words *New York* across the top first. I laughed out loud when I realized it was a crop top. He endlessly made fun of them, even though secretly he loved when I wore them.

"We leave tomorrow morning."

"Leave?" Maybe my brain was tired, but it took a minute

for me to put it all together. "We're going to New York? To see the big tree?"

He nodded, a grin breaking out across his tired face.

I walked over to him and straddled his lap, then molded my lips to his.

"I got you something else too." Placing my hands on his solid chest, I pushed off and left the room, returning a few minutes later with his wrapped present in my hands.

I was suddenly nervous about it. He patted his leg, and I swallowed before sitting across his lap.

He unwrapped the gift and flipped through it, silence stretching on forever before he raised his gaze to mine.

"A recipe book?"

I nodded. "It has some of your mom's favorites—some she said were your favorites, and some of mine too. A bunch we've tried together. And a handful from my mom as well." I squirmed as his gaze stayed locked on me. "I, um, thought we could add to it. Make some of them together. And with Sophia too."

He cocked a brow. "Sophia?"

"Yeah." I let my eyes trail down to where the first few buttons of his Henley were undone. The intricate mountain and lake tattoo were just barely visible. "If you decide to move forward with the foster and adoption process, I'm on board too."

He tangled a hand in my hair, tugging slightly, eliciting a moan from me and forcing me to meet his eyes. "Ash—"

"I know it's a big commitment and we shouldn't go into it lightly, but I want you to know that I'm open—"

Any further words were silenced when he crashed his mouth to mine.

"I love you so fucking much, princess," he rumbled against my neck as he trailed his warm lips down my throat, his hands already lifting my sweater.

"I love you too, Jackson." I giggled as he sent my top flying. "Do you think it'll always be like this?"

"Hmm?" he asked, moving my hair out of the way before sucking and biting on the skin below my ear.

"This can't get enough, even when we're exhausted, desperate for each other feeling?"

"Yes."

I pulled back, the corner of my mouth turning up into a grin. "That confident, huh?"

"I can't imagine a world where I won't constantly want you. Can you?"

I shifted so I was straddling him again. "No."

"There you go." He snapped open the front clasp of my bra. "Now, can we finish what we started? I need to be inside you, and then we both need sleep. We have a flight to catch tomorrow morning."

"Yes, Jackson. Take me to bed."

I wrapped my legs tightly around his waist as he picked me up and carried me toward the bedroom.

It was surreal. This was my life now. In the arms of this man. A man I thought I hated only a few months ago.

I wanted every single night to end like this. Forever.

Epilogue

JACKSON

SUNLIGHT FILTERED in through the windshield of my new SUV and glinted off the two-carat rock that sat on Ashley's left hand. I'd wanted to check something else off her bucket list, so I had surprised her with a trip to Italy two months ago and had proposed while we were there.

"Then Claire said he's such a Slytherin because he did none of the work and we had to do it all and it was a group project so he should have helped." Sophia took a quick breath from the back seat.

Sophia had finally been placed with us three weeks ago, and it still amazed me how easily she'd settled in. Once we were married, we could proceed with the adoption application.

"Wait a minute—who's Claire again?" I said, searching my

memory for the names she had rattled off in the last ten minutes.

"She's my friend. She loves *Harry Potter* as much as I do, and science is her favorite subject, too, and we both love cherries."

Ashley smiled before glancing back at Sophia. "Just not on ice cream sundaes, right?"

"Right, that's just weird."

We all laughed as I pulled into Ashley's parents' driveway.

Sophia jumped out of the car and ran toward the house before Ashley and I even had our doors open. I shook my head at her excitement. She had been around some members of the Williams family individually over the last few weeks, but this would be her first Sunday dinner. We'd spent the first few weekends together in our small family unit, doing our best to make sure she felt comfortable before overwhelming her with the masses.

The noise and chaos of this large, loud family hit me as soon as we stepped inside.

Sophia's eyes darted everywhere.

"You okay? Is this too overwhelming?"

She huffed. "Um—have you ever been to Dani's house?"

Yeah, she had a point. Dani's house was always as loud and chaotic as this. Maybe more so at times.

Brendan ran past us and into the living room before jumping up on the sofa where Bella sat with a now very upset baby Hudson.

"Brendan, careful of your brother," Rhett said where he stood off to the side, speaking to Kyle.

"Please tell me those aren't wedding magazines." Ashley huffed and walked over to Hattie and Savannah, who sat in side by side armchairs, flipping through what did, in fact, look like a catalog of some sort.

Hattie's smile widened as she looked up. "Wedding

dresses. We've circled a few for you to look at." She scooted over and patted the space in the chair next to her, welcoming Sophia to come sit. My heart soared as Sophia squeezed in next to her without hesitation.

"I still can't believe you snagged that one. I knew I should've called dibs years ago," Savannah chimed in with a nod in my direction.

"Stop reminding me." Rhett groaned.

I chuckled at the scene. Ashley and I might never have biological children, but I knew I wanted a family just like this. A full house. Loud, funny, and chaotic. I scanned once more, searching for my parents, who I knew were already here since we'd parked behind their car.

"Here, let me see my nephew." Kyle scooped the fussy newborn into his arms. He smiled down at the baby, the corners of his mouth almost reaching his eyes for the first time since he'd been injured.

"*Shit*," Ashley whispered, coming to stand next to me. "I'm going to owe Hattie drinks at Mamacita's, aren't I?"

"Yeah, I think you will." I tilted my head, continuing to observe Kyle, who up until a couple of weeks ago was still a miserable grump. He'd had so many changes in his life, but maybe the most recent one was exactly the one he needed. "But I told you then not to take that bet."

"Jackson," my father called from the entrance of the dining room. "Come in here. I was telling George about that marina you're thinking of investing in."

I blinked and followed behind Ashley. Before she disappeared through the barn door that stood partly open, allowing a glimpse of our moms moving around the kitchen, I grabbed her hand. I pressed my lips to hers quickly before letting my thumb skate over her engagement ring and releasing her.

A year ago, this all seemed impossible—I was a single guy trying to adopt a ten-year-old girl and wasn't convinced I'd ever find a partner. But Ashley and Sophia were the last two puzzle pieces I'd needed to make my life complete.

***

Want to see more of Ashley and Jackson?
Start at the beginning and read the first book in the series!
<u>Always Yours</u>

***

Ready to find out who finally made the grump smile?
Keep reading for a sneak peek of <u>Imperfectly Yours</u> now!

Chapter One

TINA

"Ow, Teddy. Stop pulling my hair." I hoisted my four-year-old son higher on my hip. The bulky life vest he wore made the task a little awkward. "You know I don't like that."

"I sorry."

Maybe he was. But it wouldn't stop him from doing it again. We'd had a good day, the three of us, with minimal crying and pouting. Now I hoped to make it home without another tantrum.

Doing my best to hold on to my patience, I set him on the seat at the back of the boat.

"Mom?" Behind me, my daughter was probably still sitting on the cushions at the front of the boat. It was her favorite spot.

Teddy tugged at his Puddle Jumper, trying to free an arm. "Imma take this off now?"

Luckily, he didn't know how to get himself out of it. He wasn't a fan of the water and had no interest in getting in the lake, but that didn't stop me from ensuring that he was strapped in tight while on the boat.

"Not until we're off the pier. Remember?" I tapped the turtle on the front of the floatie. "You love Thomas the turtle. You don't want him to be sad, right?"

He looked down, contemplating my question, and huffed. "Okay."

"Mom, I can't find it." Callie's voice rose two octaves.

I turned, finding her wide, tear-filled eyes on me. I wasn't sure what had happened in the last five minutes to cause this reaction, but with Callie, I had to piece together what caused her emotional swings. Just last week, she burst into tears at the park because a little boy was playing with army men.

I glanced over my shoulder at Teddy. He was still sitting, waiting patiently for me, so I took a deep breath and headed for my daughter. We'd had two good hours on the lake, but now that we were back at the dock, I was ready to get off this boat.

I took her hands in mine and kept my voice calm. "Callie, look at me, baby. What's wrong?"

"I can't find my bracelet." Her eyes swung from me to the cushion beside her to the floor, then back to the cushion like she hoped it would magically appear. "I lost it."

"It's okay." She had it when we got on the boat, so it had to be here somewhere. "We'll find it."

Showing her I wasn't worried was the first step in preventing her from spiraling.

"It's the paracord one." She shook her wrist in my face like I wasn't familiar with the bracelet she'd worn every day for the last six years. "The one daddy made me."

I smiled at the thought of it. She never took it off. She even slept with the dang thing. Something we had in common. My gaze instinctively moved to the matching one I wore on my right wrist.

"Okay, let's look for it. Did you check inside your bag?" I nodded to the mermaid tote at her feet.

"No." She sniffled.

"You look in your bag, and I'll check the cushions and floor. Deal?"

She nodded and slid to the floor, and I turned and searched the seats. Almost instantly, my fingers brushed against it as I ran a hand between two cushions.

Thank goodness. Another crisis averted.

"Found it," I called, holding it out to her.

Over her shoulder, movement caught my attention. A tall man was rushing down the pier, a scowl on his face.

I glanced over at the other slips, searching for the source of his intense frustration. But I saw nothing out of the ordinary. Did that mean it was directed at me? What could I have done to cause his irritation?

Kyle freaking Williams hadn't so much as looked my way since we'd moved to Half Moon Lake almost two months ago. And now he seemed intent on burning a hole through me with that glare of his.

When people around here found out we'd moved from Fort Bragg, the first question they asked was whether I knew Kyle Williams. Apparently, he had been stationed there as well. Clearly, they didn't realize that Fort Bragg had the largest population of any army base in the US. Over a hundred thousand soldiers and families lived and worked on that base.

Regardless, my answer was always no. I did not know the town's grumpy army vet.

So why was he eyeing me with so much fury right now? What did I do?

Before I could give it more thought, the scowl marring his face morphed into sheer terror, and he set off at a run. An instant later, there was a loud splash from the back of the boat.

I spun at the sound, and my stomach bottomed out. The spot where I had left my son was empty, except for his discarded Puddle Jumper.

"Teddy—" Stomach dropping, I bolted toward where I'd left him.

The world around me slowed to an excruciating pace. Kyle ran down the decking past the boat and dove into the water. He disappeared, and all I could do was watch helplessly. I dug my fingers into the cushions as I leaned over the back of the boat, searching the surface of the water.

I didn't even have a second to truly panic before he popped up with my son tucked into his right side. Teddy was coughing and sputtering but seemingly okay.

Without even glancing in my direction, Kyle swam toward the rocky shore. Pushing his thick blond hair out of his face, he hoisted Teddy up onto the grass, then stood and climbed out of the water.

"Come on, Callie." I helped my daughter off the boat, and we hurried down the pier. "Oh my God. Thank—"

Kyle, gray T-shirt plastered to his heaving chest, spun to face me, his eyes narrowing and his lips tightening into a scowl.

"What the hell?" He shifted my son in his arms, and with a wince, readjusted so he was holding him on his right side.

I didn't understand what his issue was, and I wasn't sure I cared as I closed the distance between us. I was trying to thank the man for his help, and here he was, acting like I'd done something wrong.

Maybe I wasn't winning a mother of the year award, but I was only one person, and I was doing the best I could.

Ready to see what happens next?
Preorder Imperfectly Yours now!

Note from the Author

Dear Reader,

THANK YOU for reading *Impossibly Yours*. I fell in love with Ashley and Jackson's story while I was writing Rhett and Bella's. The passion that burned between them and the way I saw them soften to each other spoke to me throughout the process. Neither character is meant to be perfect, but together they *are* perfect.

I appreciate each and every one of you. It's only because people like you read our books that authors like me get to publish them.

Are you curious about Jackson's sister, Brittney, and how her *new boss* worked out? Keep reading for an inside look at *Wishing to Be Yours*. A steamy, office romance novella.

Check out my website for bonus content and stay up to date with latest releases. Can you guess who the next Williams sibling is?

Love AJ Ranney

Wishing to be Yours

CHAPTER 1

Brittney

"March your uptight ass over to the bar and have a guy buy you a drink," Savannah said, crossing her arms and cocking an eyebrow at me. "If you don't, I'll make you sing karaoke tomorrow night."

Nope. No fucking way. My brother might've had the voice of an angel, but I sounded like a cat being skinned alive, and the little pain in my ass knew it. Savannah and her stupid bets.

"How—I mean—I've never..." I didn't know the first thing about getting a guy to buy me a drink.

My friends thought my lack of experience with the opposite sex was funny. I found it annoying. It wasn't purposeful, per se, but I'd spent the last eight years focused on school. I'd been in a couple of relationships, but I hadn't had time or the opportunity to do the whole single and dating thing.

Savannah laughed and shook her head before raising her shot glass in the air. "Here's to getting laid tonight."

She winked, and I struggled to remember why we were

best friends as she tossed back her shot and slammed the glass down on the table.

I rolled my eyes at her before throwing back my own shot. It burned more than I thought it would.

"*You* might be getting laid tonight. I will *not* be."

A shiver ran through me as a chilly gust of air blew in from the lake. Even the heat lamps scattered between the tables didn't stop the cool wind from breaking through.

Savannah's gaze flitted back inside, scanning the patrons that milled around the bar. "Maybe some good dick is what you need to loosen up."

Rachel, a friend I worked with at the PR firm, giggled from the other side of our high-top table. We were seated at the edge of the patio, closest to the water. I couldn't argue with the need to loosen up. It was why I was here at The Silver Lining bar in Lake Tahoe. With my current stressful work situation, getting away was exactly what I needed. What I *didn't* need was casual, mediocre sex.

"I don't do random hookups. You know that. Sex is awkward enough. I can't imagine what it would be like with someone I don't even know."

"If sex is awkward, you aren't doing it right." Savannah shook her head at me. "I probably wasted a wish on you."

"What?" My gaze trailed over her shoulder to the bar inside. It was surrounded by walls covered with dollar bills. The idea reminded me of wishing on dandelions as a kid, putting a wish out into the universe and hoping somehow it came true. According to Savannah, a person puts a wish on a dollar bill and then pins it to the wall. When it falls, the magic of the universe will make it come true.

Yeah, okay.

Savannah was many things, and although sappy wasn't one of them, she was always rooting for the impossible. So believing in rare miracles was right up her alley. Me? I thought life was what a person chose to make it. The universe and magic had nothing to do with it.

"I was just telling Shawn—" Savannah started.

"Wait, who's Shawn?" Rachel glanced around, her attention darting from one man to another, reminding me of one of those bobble heads.

Savannah rolled her eyes in her usual dramatic fashion before running one hand through her short blond locks. "The bartender." She nodded over at a dark-haired man leaning over the bar talking to a guy in a suit. "I was telling him that Brittney *really* needs to get out of her head, let go, and have fun for a change, so maybe he could put my dollar up there gingerly."

"Hey, I have fun." Even as I said the words, I knew that in the last year or so, my life had been far from fun.

I'd skipped a bachelorette weekend last month because of work. And Savannah would *not* let me forget how much fun I'd missed while they celebrated her sister-in-law's final days as a single woman. Honestly, if Savannah hadn't planned for us to fly out on a Friday and fly back on Sunday evening, she probably wouldn't have talked me into this trip either. My job was more than demanding at times, and with the recent implosion of our owner's relationship, it was even more so. It had been hard enough taking the afternoon off to travel today.

Her eyes sparkled with mischief. "Since you're so good at having fun, you'll agree to my *fun* bet, right?"

"Bets with you never work out in my favor."

She laughed. "Yeah, 'cause you're lame. But if you win, I'll let you drag me on one of those hiking trails you wouldn't shut up about on the plane."

"Who comes to Lake Tahoe and doesn't want to take in the beautiful scenery?"

"Someone who wants to drink, gamble, relax, and maybe have no-strings-attached sex. That's who. If I wanted to hike,

I'd stay home and do that with one of my three siblings who likes that shit."

Savannah knew someone who'd rented a house here, and she got us a deal for the weekend. That was why we were here. She had no interest in taking in any sights.

We were different in so many ways, but she had been my lifeline when I'd had to start over in a new place and at a new school. My parents moved my brother and me from New York City to Half Moon Lake, North Carolina, when I was ten. Savannah was the first kid to befriend me on the playground. Her carefree personality helped me feel braver. She had a knack for pushing me out of my comfort zone.

Despite her best efforts, I always found a way back into that comfort zone. When was the last time I did something crazy? Something fun?

"I don't know—I just have to get a guy to buy me a drink, right?" I asked, determined to feed off her sense of adventure. I could let loose for one night, couldn't I? It was times like this when I envied her ability to let everything go and just be.

Her eyes lit up like it was Christmas morning.

Shit. What had I gotten myself into? "It can't be sex with a stranger. That's never gonna be me."

Her face fell, and she turned to look back inside the bar.

"Okay, fine." Her attention landed back on me. "You see tall, dark, and handsome in a suit at the bar? The one who's looking over here?"

I glanced that way, heat creeping up my neck and into my cheeks when I locked eyes with the gorgeous stranger. I nodded at my friend, wishing I could run away.

"Oh, yum," Rachel said as she too took in the sexy guy who continued to hold my gaze. "I'll take your place if you chicken out."

I sent her a glare. Why was I friends with these two again?

My stomach flipped, and my nerves ratcheted up a notch.

What if the guy at the bar wasn't interested? Goodness, I'd gone up against my fair share of male clients, judges, and other attorneys. Surely, I could do this. And so what if he wasn't interested?

The cranberry and vodka I'd been sipping since we got here scraped across the tabletop as Savannah moved it closer to me.

"Liquid courage." She smirked.

I wrapped my fingers around the glass and downed the rest of the drink, this time savoring the burn.

I could do this. It was just a drink. And with a guy I'd never see again.

More by A J Ranney

Always Yours
Wishing to be Yours
Impossibly Yours
<u>Imperfectly Yours</u>

WRITING AS GRACIE YORK

Goldilocks and the Grumpy Bear
Tumbling Head Over Heels
Along Came The Girl
Peter Pumpkined Out

Acknowledgments

Like always, I need to thank my husband first. He has been one of my biggest cheerleaders, is always willing to listen to what I write, and has done bedtime with the kids more times than I probably realize. I appreciate your eagerness to help me when I'm stuck and your willingness to let me read to you.

And then to my kids, who are always curious about what Mommy is writing. And yes, you still need to wait until you're eighteen to read them. But by then I doubt you'd want to!

Jenn, I know you're sick of my stories by the time we get to this part! Regardless, thank you for dealing with my constant *how do I fix this?* questions and talking me down every time I'm ready to burn everything I write. You're always willing to read and edit multiple times, hold my hand when I need it, and tell me to just do it when I need that too. But above everything you've done, your friendship has meant the world to me.

Katie, you are amazing. Thank you for reading, for your amazing feedback, and for helping make this story everything it is!

A HUGE thank you to my author friends who have supported me in so many ways, whether through encouragement or reading my stuff: Annie Charme, Kat Long, Raleigh Damson, Jenni Bara, Brittanee Nicole, Sara Tallary, JL Reed, Dallas Ryan, Kristin Lee and many more!

Special thank you to Erica—you are the blurb master!

Beth, thank you for being so flexible, your edits, and the millions of questions, hand holding, and messages.

Haley, thank you for all the many ways you assist me. From graphics to sharing and promoting and all the stuff you likely will do that I just don't know yet. Thanks for making things easy for me so I can focus on writing.

Holly, as always, thank you for being my sister, even if not by blood—and to my mom and mother-in-law: You have been so supportive throughout every step of this crazy journey!

And finally, thank you to the rest of my friends and family who have helped or supported me. I used to think it took a village to raise little humans, and that still holds true, but it also takes a village to write and publish a book!

About the Author

A.J. Ranney lives in Maryland with her ever-growing zoo, including two kids, two cats, an attention-loving dog, a bunny, a cricket-eating lizard, and her lovable, well-meaning husband. She likes to leave the chaos of her real world behind and lose herself in a steamy romance novel. Her passion for reading romance prompted her writing journey, leading her to create relatable happily ever afters that come from her own dreams and experiences.

She loves coffee, sushi, wine, and her family. Not necessarily in that order. Her inner peace comes from the water, always relating to her zodiac sign, the Pisces. It's no wonder the small town she created in her stories is situated on a lake.